RESORTING
to
LOVE

6-24-11
To Lee + Julia

Best Wishes

Lori Rol

LORI ROHRER

A NOVEL

RESORTING
to
LOVE

TATE PUBLISHING & *Enterprises*

Published by Tate Publishing & Enterprises, LLC
127 E. Trade Center Terrace | Mustang, Oklahoma 73064 USA
1.888.361.9473 | www.tatepublishing.com

Tate Publishing is committed to excellence in the publishing industry. The company reflects the philosophy established by the founders, based on Psalm 68:11,
"The Lord gave the word and great was the company of those who published it."

Book design copyright © 2011 by Tate Publishing, LLC. All rights reserved.
Cover design by Rebekah Garibay
Interior design by Chelsea Womble

Published in the United States of America

ISBN: 978-1-61777-365-5
1. Fiction, Christian, Romance
2. Fiction, Christian, General
11.03.29

CHAPTER ONE

Everything old is new again, she thought as she looked over the agenda.

When Trisha Sterling was hired to be the director of For the Love of Family, the new, old idea in family resorts, she had no idea what was in store for her. The board of directors of For the Love of Family had decided to bring back the idea of the extended family vacation. They were hoping that it would be the latest and greatest in family get-a-ways. The idea was for families or couples to be dumped in the middle of Nebraska, miles from nowhere for six weeks. For the guests, the only way in or out was by some form of mass transit. The plan was to bring the guests into the resort by bus or something other than their personal vehicles. The guests would be offered every kind of entertainment imaginable—everything from horseback riding to miniature golf to concerts to climbing towers to rodeos and circuses. This was not a vacation for the poor or the faint of heart. It cost a pretty penny to spend six weeks at For the Love of Family. There were also wireless Internet connections for those who couldn't stand to be separated that much from the real world or at least not for that long anyway.

While it wasn't cheap to come to For the Love of Family for six weeks, neither did it run to the luxurious. The board of directors was going for a much more nostalgic feel. They wanted parents to bring their children here and be able to reminisce about what it was like for them to go to summer camp as kids. It was their hope that families would be able to share these experiences together and to create new opportunities for families with some more modern stuff too. It really was designed to be a family atmosphere, one that encouraged families to grow closer to one another. The resort was not touted as being a Christian resort, but they weren't going to complain if the guests drew closer to

God in the process. They had already put a strong Christian woman in charge.

Trisha's family had never gone on vacation together, much less a six-week one. She and her family had never been particularly close, but she had always enjoyed being around people, kids especially. At twenty-six, she was a very successful woman, largely of her own making. She had been the director at one of the church camps and was very involved with the youth organizations through her own church.

She was thrilled to be working with her best friend, Michelle Ewing. The governing board had told Trish that she could choose whomever she wanted as her assistant. There was no question whom she would choose.

Trish and Michelle had met in business management classes six years ago. They immediately became great friends. Michelle was also a strong Christian woman. They had even shared an apartment together briefly. Business management had been a good choice, a very good choice. And now Trisha owned her own house. She and Michelle were still great friends and spent a lot of time together, but they had never worked together.

"Really?" Michelle could hardly contain her excitement as she found out that she would be working with Trish. "We finally get to work together?"

"Really! They said I could pick anyone I wanted to be my assistant, and I don't know anyone more qualified." Michelle had graduated at the top of her class, with Trisha a very close second. Both were very successful in their chosen areas, Trisha with church camps and Michelle more inclined toward office management. But what Trisha had in mind wasn't so much of an assistant position as a co-director position. This project was very involved and was going to require more than Trisha could give it on her own.

Trisha had been planning and meeting for months and months to make sure everything was in place for the very first session. The first session was scheduled to start in just six weeks, and there was still quite a bit of work to do: confirmations to be made all across the board—the guests, the staff, and the venders. There were still the food arrangements to finalize. There would, of course, be an access road for deliveries and staff use.

And the rooms weren't quite ready yet either. They still needed painting and the little finishing touches. The families or couples would be staying in something very similar to a hotel economy suite. The beds even had memory foam mattresses. They would have refrigerators, microwaves, coffee makers, and hair dryers, but no stoves or ovens. They would also have some dishes and flatware. There would be a gift shop-convenience store, and laundry services available on the premises and a large dining hall where the masses would gather to spend quality family time over a meal.

"Please, Lord, could we keep the food fights to a minimum?" she wondered aloud, causing Michelle to look up from her work.

"What did you say?" Michelle asked.

She and Michelle shared an office both at the planning center and also at the resort. That made coordinating everything so much easier.

"Nothing. Just thinking out loud," she responded. "Michelle, where are we on the rock wall and the concert lineup?"

Michelle scratched her chin and hit some keys on her computer. "The concerts are all set. The guests should be very well entertained. The rock wall..." She trailed off.

After a long and drawn-out silence, Trish said, "The rock wall?" prompting Michelle to continue speaking. Michelle sometimes would get so deep in thought that she would forget she was talking. Trish really hoped that was the case now.

Michelle looked at Trish for a very long moment, and Trish felt her heart sink. "Well...they aren't going to be able to install it until two days before we open. I'm sorry."

Trish wasn't sure whether she was more frustrated or disappointed. *Two days before? That's going to be close.* She had hoped to be able to try out the rock wall for herself well before the guests arrived. *Well, I guess we'll have to see,* she thought. Otherwise, it sounded like everything was falling into place nicely. *Good. That was very good.* Even though she didn't get along with her own family, she really wanted this project to succeed.

In addition to the things that still needed done for the resort itself, there were still arrangements

to be made for her house, mail, bills, etc. Thank God she didn't have any pets to have to arrange care for. She and Michelle would be moving out to the resort in three weeks' time to oversee all the final preparations. While the guests would stay in an area that resembled economy hotel suites in layout, the staff would be staying in dormitory-style cabins. But she and Michelle would each have their own cabin with all of the amenities of home.

CHAPTER TWO

She and Michelle arrived at the resort right on time. They had brought Trisha's SUV out so that they would have plenty of room to carry everything. They stood at the entrance of the resort. It was breathtaking to see what all they would be in charge of for the next several weeks and months. The surrounding area was absolutely beautiful; there were so many trees and flowers of all descriptions. And since it was early May, everything was just coming into bloom and smelled as fragrant as it looked. The cottonwood trees were in full bloom with all of their cotton fragments floating through the air. There were also a lot of open areas where families could play or couples could walk. Trails for walking or hiking wound in and out of all of it. The

goldenrod would be blooming in a short time as well. *Hmmmm. I need to make sure the gift shop has a lot of allergy medicine in stock.*

"Where should we start?" Michelle asked quietly with awe in her voice, bringing Trish back to the moment.

Trish was still trying to take it all in herself. "Let's start with a tour, and then we'll unload. Maybe I can pull up closer to where we need to unload everything," she said, not at all sure where they should start. Of course, she and Michelle had both been given maps of the area many weeks ago, but to see it in person was a lot different. It wasn't nearly this spacious on the maps.

They believed that both the layout of the resort and the activities had been planned very well. The activities had been planned in such a way that there would be a major activity only every other week. The same venue would be used for all of these. They would end each session with a concert from a known band. The other concerts would be with up-and-coming artists. In between the concerts of each session, there would be other activities. Not every session would contain all of the same activities. There would be a rodeo, a circus, and a comedy show, all at various times during the summer. Not all of the activities would run at the same time. While some activities were in progress, like the shooting range, others would be closed, like the miniature golf course. And during the major events, most activities would be closed. They would, however, offer smaller activities for those who may not be interested in attending the major event. These smaller activities (bingo, board games, and crafts) would require less room and staff to operate but would still provide an alternative.

The first thing they came to was the dining hall. Outside the dining hall, the landscaper had planted the flowers to spell out "welcome" with purple pansies, forming the letters against a backdrop of white begonias—very clever and attractive.

The camp-style dining hall was a log structure with vaulted ceilings. It looked big enough. It would have to be. They had one hundred people coming to the resort, not including the thirty-some staff members. The tables were round pine wood tables that would seat up to nine people. Most people would not be able to dine with just their family members. Some would have to step out of their comfort zone and meet new people. Though there were a few picnic tables around the outside of the dining hall.

"I'm getting hungry just standing here," Trish said innocently.

"You're *always* hungry," Michelle replied in the way that only a good friend could get away with.

It was true. Trish was always hungry. It was odd, really. Michelle was often amazed at the food that her friend could consume and never gain an ounce while if she just looked at something that was bad for her, she could feel her clothes getting tighter.

Trish and Michelle were alike in so many ways, mostly intellectually, but so different in others. Both women were about five foot seven, but their builds were completely the opposite. Michelle was not fat; she was, however, very solid. She could not lose weight to save her life. Trisha had a very athletic build, as if she had been involved in sports her whole life. She hadn't. And she could not gain weight. That was the one good thing she got from her mother.

Their appearances were different too. Michelle had mousy brown hair cut in a stylish bob that flattered her face nicely. And she had the most dazzling smile that Trisha had ever seen. Trish thought that Michelle was very pretty in her own way.

Trisha never thought of herself as being even remotely attractive, though other people had told her they thought she was. She had all this curly, copper red hair that refused to be tamed. It didn't matter if it was long, short, or in between; her hair did whatever it wanted. Today, it was long and pulled back in a ponytail, as it was most days.

The east end of the dining hall would be where their offices would be located. The west end would house the doctor's office and the first aid station. To the west of the dining hall was the guest housing: two different two-story buildings that were connected at either end, with stairways that branched off to the north and the south At the end of the building nearest the dining hall, the north stairs went to the dining hall, and the south ones to an open field and the area where the rock climbing wall would be, *hopefully*. At the other end of the building, the north stairs went to the mini water park, the south stairs through the woods to other activities and to the major events arena. The building on the right was for families, with larger rooms, more beds, bigger living areas, etc. For the families, each suite had either two or three bedrooms. Families were assigned accordingly. The one on the left was for the couples, and everything was on a much smaller scale, having only one or two bedrooms. The guests in this building would be assigned according to preference. Some of their "couples" were just friends or, in some cases, siblings who wouldn't want to share a room. And every suite had a pullout sofa.

In between the stairway and rock wall was the gift shop. The shelving, refrigerator units, and cash registers were all in place. It was all ready to go except for the supplies. Behind the gift shop were workout facilities and a small spa.

Trish and Michelle wandered through the guest housing, taking everything in. They didn't go into every suite, of course. But they did take note of how the suites were set up, how they were progressing, and what still needed to be done. The suites would be painted in rich, warm colors. They would be rustic in appearance and have homey touches, like handmade quilts on the beds. The appliances hadn't been delivered yet. At the far end of each floor in each building were the laundry facilities. Or for an additional weekly fee, guests could have their clothes picked up, cleaned, and returned to their suites. They would be supplied with clean bed linens and towels twice weekly.

After the walkthrough of the guest housing they walked through the mini water park.

"Oh, yeah. The kids are going to love this," Trish said thoughtfully.

"Only the kids? I can very easily see you spending all of your time here if we let you," Michelle teased.

"You mean I can't? But I thought that we were supposed to be engaging with the guests in their activities."

They both laughed as they continued on around through the miniature golf course and the main activities venue. They noticed the giant screen that had been installed. It would be used during the events so that everyone could see what was happening. But when there wasn't a major event going on, it would be used to show movies, like they used to do at the old drive-in theaters. *Do any of those even still exist?*

They walked along in companionable conversation as they went through the shooting and archery range, the horse stables, then through some of the trails and ended up at the staff cabins near the dining hall.

The staff cabins were partially hidden by all of the trees. The cabins were simple but functional. And, thankfully, there was more than one bathroom in each one. Behind these cabins was a small lake. It was completely hidden from the public eye. This was to be off limits to the guests. It was for staff use only.

Trish and Michelle's cabins were in this area too, but they were tucked away in a more secluded spot not far from the lake. Apparently the developers had decided that if Trish and Michelle were going to spend all day with these people, they deserved a little a break from them at night.

Their cabins were exactly identical. Both had a small living area and an even smaller kitchen with windows that looked out over the lake. There was a full bathroom with stackable washer and dryer. The single bedroom was the most spacious part of the whole cabin, with a queen-size bed, dresser, night-stand, and lounge chair. With windows on three sides, the view from the bedroom was remarkable and very relaxing, making them both take a minute to thank God for His beautiful handiwork. The trees were splendid in their foliage with little pink and white flowers growing up between the trees. The sunlight playing through the trees created a dappling effect on the room. They could hear the birds chirping as they were busily trying to care for their young. And through the trees, they could see the glimmer of the sun on the lake. It looked very inviting, but there was not time to enjoy it right now.

After several minutes of lounging on the bed, they decided they had better get busy. Trish pulled her truck up to the dining hall, and they unloaded everything for their office. Then they pulled up to the cabins and unloaded all of their personal stuff.

The next several days were a whirlwind of activity. The staff arrived ten days later. The orientations began. Everything fell into place just like it was supposed to. The rock wall even got installed just in the nick of time for the guests to enjoy it, even though Trish did not have time to test out.

Finally, on Sunday, three weeks after Trish and Michelle had gotten there, the day they had been preparing for was here. The guests would be arriving in just a couple of hours.

Trisha gathered the staff together for a pep rally, last-minute instructions, and an impromptu worship session.

Michelle said she would like to say a prayer for the entire group. The group fell silent as Michelle prayed for the camp staff and guests over the summer.

When she finished, the staff began cheering.

They were as ready as they were going to be.

"Okay, people, let's do this!" shouted Trish over the increasing sound of cheers.

CHAPTER THREE

The first bus pulled into the parking lot behind the dining hall, and the guests began arriving at eleven. Trish was very visible to the guests as they came around the corner of the dining hall for check in at one of the temporary registration tables. Authority oozed out of her every pore, and there was no doubt in anyone's mind who was in charge.

There were several check-in attendants, including Trish and Michelle.

"Name?" Trish said, looking at a large family.

"Atkinson," said the tall man with the curly dark hair. The Atkinsons had six kids ranging in age from two to twelve.

"Welcome. Eight of you, right?" She smiled at him as she waited for his confirmation. "You are in suite ten on the first floor at the far end of this building, right here," she said. She pointed over her shoulder. "The crib you requested has been set up in the main bedroom. Please call if you would like it set up in another room, and we'll take care of it. There is a welcome luncheon at twelve thirty in the dining hall here." She gave him a map of the facility.

"Thank you," said Mrs. Atkinson. She herded her brood toward their living quarters. Mrs. Atkinson was as tiny and petite as her husband was tall. She noticed that the youngest child was crying. Trish smiled at her, but the little girl just cried louder.

"Name?" she said again to the next person in line. She looked up into the smiling face and saw the deepest, greenest eyes she had ever seen. She didn't think emeralds could be any greener than these eyes that seemed to see right through her.

"Hindley," he said. "David Hindley," he said again when Trish didn't move.

She seemed to be in some sort of trance.

"Ma'am?" He waited a beat. Still nothing.

"Ma'am? Are you all right? Do you need some water or something?"

"What? Oh! Oh! I'm so sorry. I…was…just…. um, uh…" *Lost in those green eyes,* she thought as she stuttered. "I guess I was just taking a small vacation of my own. I'm so sorry. What did you say your name was again?" she asked as she told herself to get a grip.

"David Hindley," he said again with a smile.

As Trish came back to the present, recognition of the man's name came to her. She had gotten a phone call about him just two days ago. His parents, brother, and sister were supposed to come on the trip, but something had happened to his younger sister and they weren't able to come.

"Of course, Mr. Hindley. I'm sorry to hear about your sister. I hope she is feeling better. Is there any chance that your family could join you later on?" she asked sincerely.

"No. They were pretty adamant that they would not be able to come," he said sadly.

"Well, we're glad that you're here." She sent a beaming smile at him. "Hopefully you can make the best of your time away anyway." She checked her clipboard. "You should certainly be very comfortable. You are assigned to one of the bigger family suites: suite twenty-six, second floor, this building." There had not been any time to change his accommodations from family to single.

He thanked her and walked backward carrying his bags toward the aforementioned suite.

The remainder of the guests was checked in without incident. It was time to get ready for the luncheon, the first meal their guests would enjoy.

The luncheon was served family style. They had barbecued chicken, pasta, Caesar salad, and strawberry shortcake. Most of the meals would be served family style, but there would be times throughout that they would be able to have meals to order.

While the guests and staff were finishing their dessert, Trish climbed up on a small platform to make the welcome announcements.

"On behalf of the staff, I would like to welcome you to For the Love of Family. I am Trisha Sterling, and this is Michelle Ewing," she said, indicating Michelle, who waved at everyone. "We are the co-directors here. We hope that you will have a very enjoyable time while staying with us here. If there is anything that you need, please be sure to let either one of us or someone on the staff know." At this point, she introduced the entire staff, including the kitchen staff and the head cooks, Tom and Becky.

She also made sure to introduce Dr. Mike and his nurse, Katy. Dr. Mike had one of those last names that was tremendously difficult to pronounce. Trish had thought that Dr. Mike was kind of cute when she first saw him. He was tall and slightly skinny, with light brown hair and a gorgeous smile. But she had seen him watching Katy very carefully. She suspected there might be something between them, even if it was just in the beginning stages. Perhaps she should just leave Dr. Mike alone. She didn't really need a love interest in her life at this point in time anyway.

After the introductions, she continued on with her speech. "Michelle and I share an office." She pointed to the door to their office. "But we won't be in there very often. We're not office directors. We'll be out and about every day. Where you are is where we'll be—most of the time. I'm available anytime. This is my Nextel walkie-talkie phone, and my number is on all of the literature you were given. It's on signs on all of the phones in your suites and in every activity center, not to mention on various other signs throughout the resort. Just let me know if I can help you in any way. I also carry a regular walkie-talkie, as does all of the staff. They can always get me on it." She stopped to take a drink of her soda. She was going to have to talk louder because the youngest Atkinson child was crying again. "Keep in mind, though, that if you call me and I don't answer right away, I am human. Sometimes I have to do things like, oh, say, take a shower, brush my teeth, sleep." At this everyone laughed. She continued. "Please try again in a few minutes. If it's urgent and can't wait a few minutes, then go to the nearest staff member. Either they can take care of it or try to reach Michelle or me on the walkie-talkie.

"Michelle, do you have anything to add?" she asked.

Michelle shook her head. "No. I think you covered everything pretty well."

"Okay, then. Let's get this vacation started." She got ready to jump down from the platform, but found a strong male hand waiting to assist her down. That hand belonged to the tall, handsome frame of one David Hindley. Again she just stared at him. She quickly recovered this time.

"Thank you," she whispered.

"My pleasure," he murmured.

Just then, one of the guests needed to speak with Trisha. And with that, the spell was broken. David let go of her hand. She spoke with the guest and turned to thank him again, but he was gone.

The activities had already begun. The evening would end with a bonfire and fireworks.

CHAPTER FOUR

The next day dawned hot and humid, so typical of this time of year in Nebraska.

The staff was allowed to take their meals wherever they chose. Trish and Michelle would eat their meals in the dining hall with the guests. Today, Trish was sitting with three different couples for the noon meal. One couple was a young man and woman who were obviously crazy about each other: Jason and Megan. They were sitting at the table alone when Trish walked up and asked if she could join them. Before they were joined by the others, Trish was able to learn that they were a Christian couple. They had come to this place to spend as much time together as possible before becoming engaged. They wanted to make sure they were able to get to know each other well in a nonthreatening environment before committing their lives to each other. Trish understood perfectly what they were really saying. Both of their families were very meddlesome and would not let them have a moment's peace with each other. They were each staying in a single room.

The second couple to join the group was a pair of sisters, Babs and Frankie. They were in their late forties and very snooty. Trish was not really sure why they were here. So far they seemed to fight constantly. When they weren't fighting, they were complaining. They didn't have a nice word to say to each other or about anyone else or anything.

And the third couple was...well...different: Chris and Pat. They were very androgynous. Trish was not sure whether they were young men or women or one of each. If she were guessing, she would guess them to be in their late teens or early twenties. However, there were times she wasn't even sure they were human. She had no idea what their relationship was. Brothers? Sisters? Brother and sister? Friends? Something else? They were definitely something else, but that still did not define their relationship. Nor did she know why they were there. In her mind, she decided they would be Thing One and Thing Two, and the less she knew about them the better.

The conversation around the table during that long meal was stilted at best. Jason and Megan were cheerful and tried to carry the conversation, but Babs and Frankie kept interrupting and being rude. And Thing One and Thing Two just made odd remarks at odd times that didn't make sense to anyone.

"How long have you two known each other?" Trish asked politely of Jason and Megan.

Jason looked over at Megan. "We actually have known each other—"

"Oh, what difference does it make how long they have known each other?" Babs interrupted.

Everyone just looked at her in disbelief.

Trish glared at Babs as she spoke. "I'm sorry, Jason. You were saying?"

Jason and Megan also glared at Babs. Jason continued, "We've known each other since we were five years old, but we just recently realized how much we were attracted to each other."

"Yeah, you know, the phrase 'You were with me all the time,'" Megan said, smiling.

"My underwear is green with bowling pins on them." This came from either Thing One or Thing Two.

Again Trish just looked in disbelief, not quite comprehending what was going on.

"Well, I never!" Frankie started. "Can you believe how rude *it* is?"

"I hope the whole summer isn't going to be like this," Babs continued.

"She called you an *it*," said the other Thing, laughing and snorting.

Those four people continued talking over one another while Jason and Megan looked embarrassed, and Trish looked from one person to the other, looking for something that she had missed. *Is this really happening?* she thought.

Fortunately, Michelle walked up and asked Trish if she was ready to make afternoon rounds yet. Trish was never so glad to be finished with a meal and find an excuse to leave in all her life.

They made their rounds, starting through the open field on the way to the hiking trails, going clockwise around the resort.

The staff all reported that everything was good. No problems so far. They were off to a good start on this first full day.

Because the day was already so hot for May, the water park was very busy. They stood there for a few minutes, watching all of the activity.

Trish was wondering if she could shake Michelle and go play in the water herself.

"Don't even think about it," Michelle said, reading Trish perfectly.

Trish was hanging her head and looking crest fallen but did not answer.

Michelle laughed at her friend's forlorn expression.

They spotted the Atkinsons playing in the kiddie area. The youngest child was crying again. Trish had learned that her name was Hallie. The other Atkinson children seemed to be having a good time playing in the water. The oldest child was trying to convince his father to let him go play in the wave pool alone. He didn't appear to be winning the argument.

"Trish, do you have your sunscreen on?" Michelle whispered.

Trish found that with all of the noise of the water splashing and kids squealing in the background, she was having a difficult time hearing what was being said.

She leaned closer to Michelle. "I'm sorry. What did you say?"

Michelle spoke louder and repeated her question.

Trish was all poised to reply, "Yes, Mom, I do," but before she could get the words out, she noticed David coming out of the wave pool with his dark hair wet and slicked back. His body indicated that he was no stranger to the gym. In fact, it looked as though he spent quite a bit of time there.

And she just stood there with her mouth forming a perfect O. She could say nothing.

David walked toward them. Trish remained speechless with her mouth hanging open.

"Ladies," he said as he approached, smiling. He stopped in front of them. He seemed to want to say something, but he just stood there.

"Excuse me," he said, his grin even bigger. The women still did not know what he wanted.

Trish thought that he might be talking to her, but she couldn't hear him any better than she could hear Michelle.

"My towel." He motioned behind them, his even, white teeth showing.

Michelle finally understood what he wanted. They were standing in front of the chair that held his towel and belongings. Michelle stepped aside, but Trish continued to stand in the same place.

She finally realized what was going on when Michelle grabbed her arm. "I'm sorry. Did you say something, Mr. Hindley?" she asked. "I seem to be having a hard time hearing you."

"My towel," he said again, motioning to the chair behind her with a huge grin on his face.

She followed the direction of his hand and slowly looked at the chair behind her, dawning coming at last. Michelle had to walk a few feet away before she embarrassed Trish with her laughter.

"I'm sorry Mr. Hindley. We didn't realize we were in your way."

"Please call me David," he said, again with that huge grin on his face.

"Right. David," Trish managed, feeling embarrassed despite Michelle's efforts. "We...um....we should be going. We need to finish our rounds." She began walking backward and nearly fell over a chaise lounge, which caused David's grin to only get bigger and Michelle's laughter to be unleashed all over again.

As the women walked away, Trish teasingly slapped Michelle's arm. "Why didn't you help me?" she railed. "The man probably thinks I'm a complete idiot."

Michelle was laughing so hard by this point that she was grabbing her sides and having a hard time walking herself.

CHAPTER FIVE

The next day Trish was scheduled for a private breakfast with another pair of sisters, Annie and Bridgett Kepling. These girls were in their early twenties. They were both very pretty blondes, petite, and physically fit. Annie was five foot one and Bridgett didn't even hit the five foot mark. Annie had hair that was poker straight and green eyes. Bridgett had amber eyes and kinky curly hair almost as unruly as Trish's own. Annie was very outgoing and very personable, while Bridgett was much more shy and reserved.

Annie told Trish that Bridgett hadn't even been in the dining hall until this morning.

"If she hasn't been coming to the dining hall, how has she been getting her meals?" Trish asked.

"I come and eat my meals with others and then take some back to her in our suite. I only got her to agree to come this morning because it was going to be in your office."

The plan was that they would have breakfast together and then spend the morning together in various activities.

"So, what did you want to do today?" Trish asked as she watched Bridgett scoop up eggs as if she was starving.

Annie waited for a minute to give Bridgett a chance to answer. When she didn't, Annie spoke up, "I would like to try out the rock wall. That looks like a lot of fun. What do you think, Bridgett?"

Bridgett continued to scoop up her eggs for a second before she looked up. "Yeah, the rock wall looks like fun, but I was thinking that I would like to try the archery range," she replied hesitantly.

Finally, Trish thought, *I might get to try out the rock wall.* "Have you done either of those before?" Trish asked of Bridgett.

"I've never climbed a rock wall before. I sometimes go bow hunting with our dad."

"Really?" Trish was surprised. "I don't know that I would have the heart to do something like that," she said truthfully.

"Bridgett is a very good shot. She also shoots competitively. That's probably why Dad takes her hunting with him and not me. My aim and my follow-through are both really awful." She laughed.

"Maybe it would be best to start at the archery range then," Trish said, hiding her disappointment. Both girls agreed.

They had a delightful breakfast. And both girls really were very sweet. They were just finishing breakfast in the office when Trish got beeped on her walkie-talkie.

"Hey, Trish, Jeff here," the talkie squawked.

Trish apologized to the girls. "I'm sorry. I have to take this." The girls nodded their understanding.

"Yeah, Jeff, go ahead."

"We have a situation down at the beginning of the hiking trail that we could use your help with."

"Sure thing, Jeff. I'll be right down." She looked at the sisters. She could tell they were disappointed. "I am so sorry. Unfortunately, this is part of my job. You can go ahead and go to the archery range without me if you would like." They nodded their agreement. They were disappointed, but they understood. "Hopefully, this won't take very long and I can meet up with you later like we planned."

The girls thanked her for breakfast. As she was grabbing her walkie-talkie off the table and heading out, Trish thought she heard Bridgett say that maybe she would try the rock wall after all. Trish didn't know whether to be relieved or disappointed. If Bridgett was going to go ahead and try the rock wall, they had made some progress. But on the other hand, Trish still was not going to get her chance. *Bummer.* Oh well, she would eventually get there.

Trish walked to the hiking trail. She saw Jeff first. He was hard to miss. He had the look of a surfer just in from Malibu: blond curly hair kissed by the sun, with skin that had also been kissed by the sun, and blue eyes that were just a shade lighter than Trisha's own.

She thought she might see what the problem was before she got there, but she wasn't entirely sure. There stood Jeff and another staff member with a couple of people she had yet to meet: a middle-aged Asian woman and her father, who was in a wheelchair.

"Hey, Jeff. What's up?"

"Trish. I'm glad that you're here. This is Li Yee and her father, Kim Yee." He said, indicating the woman and then the man.

"I'm Trisha Sterling, the director here," she said as she extended her hand to the woman. "What can I help you with?" she asked the woman.

"I want to take my father on a hike, but this man won't let me," she replied.

"Ms. Yee. I'm sorry. Is your father able to walk?" she asked, concerned.

"Sure, Father can walk," she replied.

Trish was even more confused. Mr. Yee looked barely conscious, much less able to walk. "Can you help me understand why he is in the wheelchair now?"

"He can't walk very far for very long." She didn't seem to see the problem with trying to take him on a hiking trail when he couldn't walk for very long.

"Ms. Yee, how about we see how well your father can stand and walk right now while there are several of us here? If he is able to stand and walk all right, we will not only let you take him for a hike, I will personally go with you."

Li Yee agreed, and Trish motioned to Jeff and the other staffer to try to help Mr. Yee stand. They explained to the man that they wanted him to stand up. They each grabbed him under his arms and tried to help him stand. The man never made a sound. Nor was he able to help at all. He was not able to bear any weight for even a full minute, much less walk. They put him back in the wheelchair.

Trish pushed the wheelchair and led Li Yee over to a nearby bench. She had the two staffers stay within sight distance in case she would need them again but out of hearing distance so that she could talk to Li privately.

"Ms. Yee. I understand that you would like to take your father on a hike. My staff members were only looking out for the safety of you and your father. These trails are not designed to accommo-date a wheelchair. It would be very dangerous for both of you if you were to try to take the wheelchair out there." She grasped Li's hands and looked directly in her eyes with nothing but compassion. "Your father is not steady enough on his feet at this time to go on a hike with you. Maybe later in the week he can go, but I would rather that you didn't try today. I'm sorry."

Li Yee nodded and looked out over the open field, her face filled with sadness.

"They will be starting bingo in the dining room shortly. Can I help you take him down there?" Trish asked kindly.

"No. I will do it," said Li.

When Trish saw that Li and her father were indeed headed in the direction of the dining hall, she motioned for Jeff to come over to her.

"Good call, Jeff. What's the story here? Do you know?"

Jeff scratched his head thoughtfully before he answered. "The best I can tell, the old man is really sick. I'm not exactly sure what's wrong with him, but his daughter seems to think that he is healthier than he is.

"I see," she said as she watched Li struggle with the wheelchair in the field, understanding completely the sadness she had seen earlier on Li's face. "Keep an eye on them. Let me know if there are any more problems. That was a great job, Jeff."

Trish went to the archery range where she had planned to go with the Kepling sisters, but they were not there. They must have decided not to go to the archery range after all. She decided she would see if they were somewhere else before she went back to her office to see what she could find out about the Yees.

As she passed by the horse stables, she stopped to watch a couple of small boys ride the horses. She walked to the fence and stood next to their parents, John and Daphne Jones.

"Cute boys," Trish said, watching the two little dark heads as they were led around the horse arena on their mounts. "How old are they?"

Daphne just beamed. "They will be five in September."

"Twins," Trish said with a smile.

"This one in the blue shirt is Lucas, and the one in the yellow shirt is Samuel," John said.

About that time, the boys came riding up to the fence. "Mommy, Mommy, we go fast on the horses," said Lucas.

"Look how high we are," Samuel squealed.

"I see," said Daphne. "Can you say hello to Ms. Sterling?"

"Hi," the boys said in unison.

"Howdy, partners," she said in an exaggerated drawl that caused both boys to giggle.

"You talk funny," one of them told her.

"So I do," she said as she smiled at them. "Do you like the horses?" They only nodded. "Will you go to school in the fall?" she continued.

"No," said Samuel, shaking his head sadly.

"We're not big enough yet," said Lucas, mimicking his brother perfectly.

They rode off as Daphne started to answer Trish. "Where we live, they have to be five before August first in order to start school."

Trish thought for a minute. "I'm sure that I saw it somewhere, but I'm afraid that I don't remember. Where is it that you live?"

"Illinois," John replied, watching his boys on the horses. "I've just got to tell you, this is a great place you got here. We've never done anything like this before, but this is just wonderful. We may be back next year. The boys are having a great time."

"Thank you very much," Trish replied. "I appreciate that."

They watched the boys for a few more minutes before Trish finally said, "Well, I suppose I should be moseying on, tending to my chores and such. Let me know if there is anything that you need."

She continued on toward her office.

As she was passing the rock wall, she saw that Bridgett was halfway up and appeared to be having the time of her life. Trish assumed this was the first time up.

Trish approached Annie, who was standing on the ground with her harness on, waiting for her turn.

"She finally decided to try it?" she asked.

"Are you kidding? This is the only place we've been. We've been here ever since we finished breakfast. I lost track of how many times we've been up that wall," Annie said enthusiastically. "I'm so proud of her!"

Trish watched her for a moment thoughtfully. Then she decided the information about the Yees could wait a little while longer. She was going to strap on a harness and climb the rock wall with these girls just as she had originally planned to do.

CHAPTER SIX

A couple of days later, Trish was having lunch with the Atkinson clan. Today's menu consisted of spaghetti and meatballs, fruit salad, and angel food cake. Hallie Atkinson cried through the entire meal. *Did she never stop crying?*

Trish now understood why Mrs. Atkinson was so skinny after six kids. If it wasn't Hallie crying, it was one of her siblings needing something. The children, except for the two oldest ones, were all covered in spaghetti sauce. Hallie had a piece of spaghetti hanging from her ear. Trish tried to help out as much as she could, but Mrs. Atkinson seemed to have six hands and handled things well on her own.

Everything, that is, except putting food into her own mouth. When everyone else was finished and the dishes were about to be cleared, Mrs. Atkinson had hardly touched her own food. Trish felt very helpless and didn't remember having felt that way before.

After lunch, as she was making her rounds, she noticed that David was sitting on one of the benches near the hiking trail with his laptop. He appeared to be doing some work.

She approached him. "Mr. Hindley?"

He looked up at her. "David, remember?"

"Right. David, I wanted to apologize to you for the other day."

"Apologize for what?" He had a confused look on his face.

"The other day in the water play area. I must have looked like a complete idiot to you. I'm not normally. I was having trouble hearing you over the background noise."

"You don't have to apologize to me for anything. I didn't even notice anyway."

"That's kind of you to say. You know, it's not really a vacation if you work during it," she said matter-of-factly.

He looked up at her and smiled. "Guilty as charged," he replied. "I can't help myself. I've been doing this for so long that it feels wrong to not be doing it."

"I thought that your family wanted you to take some time off. Do they know that you smuggled your laptop in here?' she asked conspiratorially.

"No." He shook his head. "I would be in trouble if they knew I was working," he confessed. "Especially if my mother knew. She worries."

"Well, now, we can't let that happen, now, can we? I have an idea. So that your family doesn't find about you working and you don't have the temptation to do so, how about you let me beat you in a game of putt-putt?"

He thought for just a moment, then closed up his laptop. "You're on, but you'll not likely be winning," he told her with great confidence.

She grinned. *So he is the competitive sort. Good to know.*

"Do you want to take your laptop back to your suite? Or we could put it in my office if you would like."

"I'll take it to my suite and then meet you at the miniature golf course in five minutes."

"That's great." She called to let Michelle know of her plans.

"You're a big girl," Michelle responded. "You are also the boss, so you don't have to check in with me."

"Thank you very much, Mom. And aren't you the same person who reminded me just the other day to put my sunscreen on?" she said sarcastically. "I just wanted you to know where I would be."

She met David at the miniature golf course as planned.

They started off behind the Kendalls, a family of five with three teenagers. Simon was nineteen. Destiny was sixteen, and Jack was fourteen. Their parents, Bart and Marianne, had to work really hard to convince the kids to even come. Being teenagers, they would have much rather stayed at home to be with their friends.

Even though the kids hadn't wanted to come originally, they seemed to be enjoying themselves at the moment. Jack was winning by a landslide, and Simon and Destiny were not too happy about being beaten by their younger brother.

"You have to be cheating," Simon accused.

Destiny was quick to agree with Simon while Jack defended himself.

"I can't help it you two don't have any idea how to play," Jack said.

Bart and Marianne didn't interfere, knowing the kids weren't really fighting with each other, just teasing in the way that siblings do.

"You know, Destiny, if you paid more attention in geometry, maybe you would be able to beat Jack," Bart said.

"Right, Dad, like geometry has anything to do with miniature golf," Destiny retorted with an attitude.

Trish and David had seen the whole thing and were laughing with the family. David found that he couldn't hold his tongue any longer. "Actually, geometry does have a lot to do with this. It's all about the angles. So is billiards."

"Just whose side are you on anyway?" Destiny said, making everyone laugh even harder.

She was bound and determined to prove them wrong. She took her shot and got frustrated when the ball didn't go where she wanted it to.

"Stink," she said in frustration.

Jack, who was a wiz in math, said "I think that if I hit the ball so that it bounces off that wall at that spot, then it will go right in the cup." As if to prove his superiority, when he hit the ball, it did exactly as he predicted that it would do. Everyone cheered at his hole-in-one except for Destiny, who was pouting.

Because there were so many Kendalls and just Trish and David, the Kendalls let Trish and David go ahead of them.

David was humbled and humiliated as he tried the same shot that Jack had just taken and his shot went horribly awry. It ended up taking him four shots to put the ball in the cup.

"What was that you were saying about geometry?" Destiny teased him, reminding him so much of his own sister.

They had a great time, even though Trish beat David by a much bigger margin than even he anticipated.

To make up for beating him, they walked over to the gift shop, and she bought him some ice cream.

Trish was so busy people-watching that her ice cream melted all over her before she could eat it all. She was a mess, and David just laughed at her, feeling some redemption at the turn of events.

David reached over to help her clean up the mess. "Here, let me help you with that," he said as he tried to help her clean while trying to contain his laughter, without much success. Their eyes locked for a minute. "I ...uh ..." he began but didn't finish when she looked at him with those clear blue eyes; his hand just sort of hovered in mid-air, not really cleaning anything.

"Can you excuse me, please? I'll just run to my cabin and change my shirt."

Trish left to go to her cabin. She could feel the blush heating her cheeks. She chanced a look over her shoulder and saw that David was still watching her. Her blush deepened.

CHAPTER SEVEN

Friday was warm, but not as warm as Monday had been. Trish and Michelle enjoyed a lovely breakfast of French toast with the Kepling sisters and a couple of other staffers who routinely took their meals in the dining hall with the guests.

Trish and Michelle had just finished their morning rounds when David approached them.

"There you are," he said as he approached them.

"I'm sorry. Did you need me?" Trish asked with concern. "You should have had one of the staffers call me on the walkie-talkie," she said sincerely.

"No. It's not urgent," he replied.

"I'm going to let you two be. I've got…somewhere else to be," said Michelle. She walked away smiling.

Once Michelle had left, he spoke again. "I'm feeling the urge to work again. So I was wondering if you might be free to go on some trails with me."

"I don't have anything pressing that I need to do. Sure. I'll go with you."

They talked as they hiked. He told her all about his family. His parents owned a furniture store in the city nearest the resort—the same city that Trish herself lived in. They were fourth-generation owners. For now, David was the accounts manager, but eventually, when his parents were ready to turn over the reigns, the store would belong to him and his siblings.

He had a brother who was a junior in college and a sister who was a junior in high school.

Trish had a funny look on her face as she tried to figure out the gap in ages between David and his brother, but didn't ask about it.

As if David could read her mind, he said, "I'm twenty-nine. My parents started really young. They were both still in high school when my mother had me. But they got married, and their parents helped them out. They were able to pull their lives together before they had my brother."

Trish only nodded, a little jealous.

"My brother and I are nothing alike," he told her. "I am the serious one, and Todd is the funny one. Todd always has a slew of girls around him while I just kind of walk around like a puppy with my tail between my legs because I'm so neglected." He said it so wistfully that Trish just stared at him for a few seconds. And then she burst into laughter. David was smiling at his own joke too.

"I don't believe any of that for a minute," she told him good naturedly. "I'm fairly certain that getting girls is not a huge a problem for you."

"Well, it is and it isn't," he confessed. "I've always been able to hold my own in that area. But I work so much. I'm in the office all of the time. I don't have a lot of opportunities to socialize with the weaker sex," he teased.

"Weaker sex?" she said in mock outrage. "If memory serves me, *I* beat *you* the other day at the miniature golf course."

"I let you win."

"You *let* me win? Oh, I don't think so. I beat you fair and square, buddy."

"Of course I let you win. It was what you wanted. You asked for it."

"What I wanted? I asked for it?" she sputtered.

Before she could say anything else, David continued, "When you invited me to play, you said, 'How about you let me beat you in a game of putt-putt?'" He was laughing and his eyes were shining with amusement.

It took her a minute to remember, and then she started laughing too. She was going to have to be careful with this one. He could turn her own words against her so easily.

His sister, Chelsea, was a gymnast, a pretty serious one too. She was training for the Olympics. During one of the training sessions just a few days before the resort was to open, she had fallen off the uneven bars. She had hit her head and received a concussion. She had also broken her arm. She could have come to the resort with the broken arm, but the concussion was a different matter. David's parents thought it would be best to stay close to home just to make sure that everything was okay. Trish couldn't say that she blamed them.

David also told her about being in Boy Scouts and how much he loved the organization. He and his brother were both Eagle Scouts, as was his father. His father had been in the Air Force and was currently a deacon at their church. Their church was just down the road from Trish's own church. She was glad to know that he was a Christian man.

As they were nearing the end of the trail, he said, "Okay, you know just about everything there is to know about my family. Tell me about yours."

She hesitated. "There's really not much to tell," she said after a moment.

"Oh, come on. Everyone is embarrassed by their family occasionally. I'll bet your dad is an engineer who is wild about sports, and your mother is a manager of a very prominent company, and you have several siblings, all sisters."

She still didn't answer and looked off in the distance. It was like she was looking into the past. She looked back at him and smiled, but it was a sad smile. "Fortunately, I am an only child. My father skipped town when I was two. My mother was gone more than she was around. It was always men and drugs, drugs and men. She didn't even know that I was around most of the time. I became very good at taking care of myself."

David did not say anything but let Trish talk.

Her pace had slowed. They weren't hiking now; it was more of a meandering walk. "When I was thirteen, I lied about my age and got a job. It didn't pay more than minimum wage, but it was my money. My mother never knew. I also did whatever odd jobs I could around the neighborhood, sometimes in exchange for food. Sometimes I got paid in cash. I saved my money until I had enough. When I was fifteen, I hired a lawyer and went to court to have myself declared an emancipated minor. I have no living relatives that I know of, and I didn't want to go into the system. I didn't want foster parents. I didn't see how they could take better care of me than I could take care of myself, better care of me than I had been taking of myself." She pulled a wildflower out of the ground and shredded it as they walked. "I got an apartment. It didn't have much in it. But it was mine." She looked out over the fields again, as if she was looking into the past. "I haven't seen or talked to my mother since. I don't even know if she is still alive."

"I'm sorry. I can't imagine how rough it must have been to grow up that way."

She nodded her thanks. Her mind was still in the past. "That was a long time ago. A lot of water has gone under the bridge since then."

"So how did you meet Michelle?" he asked.

"We met in college. We hit it off instantly. We became very good friends. Her family sort of adopted me. Michelle has four brothers, and I was the sister she never had. They made me feel welcomed. They made me feel loved. I matter to them. I spend nearly every holiday with them. You know, her family is a lot like how you described yours, a lot of love for everyone. They are always willing to do whatever they can for those less fortunate, sharing whatever they have with anyone in need. They take in strays, whether they are animal or human."

"Is that what you are? A stray?" he asked with genuine concern.

"Not anymore. I was, but I'm not anymore," she said honestly. She was quiet for a minute. "Shortly after I became an emancipated minor, a friend at school asked me to go church with her. I started going to church with her on a regular basis. I realized that as independent as I was, I couldn't do it alone. And God didn't want me to do it alone. I discovered that He loves me, and He wants me to call on Him when I need help. I'm not to try to walk the path alone. It was comforting and strange to know that someone somewhere loved me, even though I surely didn't deserve it. I still don't, but He loves me anyway. One of my favorite verses is John 3:16: 'For God so loved the world that He gave his only begotten son, that whosoever believes in Him should not perish but have everlasting life.' He loved me so much that He was willing to give all he had to save me. And He promises me a place to live forever. I will never have to feel like I don't belong in His family. I had never experienced love of any kind before and certainly not this sacrificial kind."

"That is one of my favorites too. It's good to be reminded of God's love for us. He also says in Mathew that he will provide for us and that we are not to worry about what we will eat or where our clothes will come from. I'm just curious, what did you do for food and clothes?"

"He was true to His word. The church was very helpful. I got a lot of meals from them and food items. I learned to cook and to do with whatever was at hand. I became very creative with recipes. I also got hand-me-downs, so I learned to sew. I could take nearly any clothing that was given to me and turn it into something else that was more fitting and flattering to me, even boys' clothes. The church was the support system I never had at home."

They continued to walk while she continued to shred the wildflower.

"You seem to be a very educated woman. How were you able to go to college?"

Trish grinned a little. "No one ever accused me of being dumb," she said with a light in her eyes. "I was the valedictorian of my high school class and the salutatorian of my college class. Michelle was valedictorian. Not that there was anyone there to see it." She was looking into the past again. "There were members of the church there, of course. Since I had the grades and was an emancipated minor, I qualified for several scholarships. And, again, the church did all they could do to help. I don't do anything by myself anymore. But for the grace of God, there go I."

She had stopped briefly and smiled then, a real smile, one that reached all the way to her eyes.

As she stepped back to turn so that they could continue their walk, she tripped over a tree root and stumbled. His reflexes were quick, and he reached out and grabbed a hold of her arms, pulling her to him and steadying her. Their eyes met and locked. They leaned toward each other. Trish was sure he was going to kiss her, and she was ready, anticipating.

"Trish, we have a situation at the wave pool. We need you right away," her walkie-talkie squawked. "It's the Yees again."

Trish and David looked at each other for just a second. Both let out a heavy sigh, and Trish said, "I've got to go."

David nodded and kissed her forehead just before she turned and broke into a run to go the wave pool.

Out of breath from the run, Trish arrived at the wave pool to find Mr. Yee half in, half out of his wheelchair. One of the lifeguards was standing by. She motioned for the lifeguard to assist Mr. Yee to get back into the wheelchair.

Before she could say anything, Li Yee told her, "My father wants to go for a swim."

Trish was incredulous. Mr. Yee was nearly catatonic. There was no way he was going to be going for a swim. He wasn't even wearing swim trunks. In fact, he was wearing the same clothes he had been wearing a couple of days ago when Trish saw them on the trail. Trish began to wonder if Li was really capable of taking care of her father. Clearly she was not able to transfer him very well. Trish had dealt with them twice in less than a week's time, and both times he had nearly fallen and would have if her staff members had not stepped in to assist. *Does she bathe him? Does he ever get out of the wheelchair, or does he sleep there too?*

Trish tried the same approach as before. "Ms. Yee, how well is your father able to walk today?"

"Good," said Li vaguely.

"Can you tell me specifically what activities he has been able to do by himself today?" Trish asked compassionately.

"He took a shower, got dressed, and walked to breakfast," she said, never making eye contact with Trish at all.

Trish took a deep breath before she began. "Ms. Yee. Are you sure he did all of those things by himself? Today?"

"Yes," she said, but she still wouldn't look at Trish.

"Ms. Yee," she started slowly. "I can't imagine how difficult this is for you. I know that he is the only family you have left. It is admirable that you want to spend so much time with him in his golden years. But I don't believe that he did any of those activities by himself today. I saw him at breakfast this morning. He was in his wheelchair. I think that these are the same clothes he had on the other day, and I know that you tried to feed him this morning. I don't understand how he could have been stable enough to do all that you say he did, and then in just a few minutes' time be unable to even feed himself." She looked at Li with compassion and sympathy.

Li was beginning to cry softly as Trish again held onto her hands and looked in her eyes.

"Your father can not swim with you today," she said softly. "You need to find a different, less physical activity for you and your father to participate in."

Li nodded as tears rolled down her face.

Trish watched with sadness as the woman pushed her father back toward their suite. She wondered how much time Mr. Yee had left on this earthly plane and where he would spend eternity. She didn't know if she could talk to Li about it without sending her completely over the edge. And Mr. Yee certainly was not going to tell her. She was going to have to figure out how to talk to Li about it.

Later that night was their first concert. Trish stood along the back wall enjoying the concert with a couple of the other staff members. She watched the Kendalls picking on one another as they had done during the miniature golf game. She watched the adorable Jones boys as they bounced up and down in their seats, having never been to a concert before. She was pleased to see Annie and Bridgett enjoying the concert and not at all surprised that neither Babs and Frankie or Thing One and Thing Two were there.

The band was into their third song when David approached her.

"Are you planning to stand through the whole concert?"

She smiled at him. "Yes, it gives me more opportunity to watch over everything else. I can also leave more easily without disturbing others if I'm needed somewhere else."

David did not move.

Wanting to see that he was comfortable and enjoying the show, she continued. "The seats down there are much more comfortable than this wall is," she said, pointing to the area he had just come from.

"Maybe," he said slowly. "But I usually enjoy concerts more when there is a beautiful woman next to me."

She blushed and looked around her to see whom he might be talking about.

He noticed and chuckled. "I was talking about you. You don't take compliments very well, do you?" Well, after all that she had shared with him earlier in the day, he shouldn't be so surprised.

"I would like to enjoy the concert with you," he said quietly as Trish blushed again. "If you are going to stand here to watch the concert, so am I," he said with all sincerity. He smiled at her, then turned and leaned against the same wall she was leaning against with his arms folded across his chest, tapping his foot in time to the music with a big smile on his face.

CHAPTER EIGHT

The next week passed without incident. Well, without major incident, anyway. Thing One and Thing Two had been banned from the miniature golf course for destruction of some of the props, which had had to be repaired, and for breaking two of the clubs, which had had to be replaced. They had also been banned from the shooting range for not following instructions.

Trish spent time with David during the day when she could, which was not often, since she had to be available to all of the other guests too. But they spent every evening after dinner together. Even though they spent every evening together in different activities, he had not tried to kiss her again. She thought that maybe she had misread his interest in her.

It was Friday again. She had breakfast with the Atkinsons. Hallie was still crying. She had scrambled eggs everywhere. The other children did much better with their breakfasts. They definitely did better with scrambled eggs than they had with the spaghetti. Mrs. Atkinson still didn't get much opportunity to eat. *Poor woman,* Trish thought. Trish was not the least bit jealous of Mrs. Atkinson's small frame; she was worried and amazed at it. *How did this small body manage to support this woman and all that she was able to do without getting much food into it?*

This was one day that Trish was able to spend with David. After breakfast they went to the shooting range where they spent a couple of hours.

"You know, when I was in the Boy Scouts, I got a merit badges in rifle and shot gun shooting." David sounded confident in his abilities.

"Is that so?"

"Yeah." He took his first shot and missed.

Trish didn't say anything as she took her first shot and hit the mark perfectly.

"That was a lucky shot." David took another shot and hit the target slightly off center.

"Okay, if you say so." Her next shot hit the mark perfectly center again.

They continued on this way the entire time they were at the shooting range. Trish could see that she had surprised him with her accuracy.

For a woman who hadn't had many experiences as a child, she seemed to be good at just about everything.

"What was that you said about the weaker sex?' she asked innocently with a glimmer in her eye.

"How is it that everything you touch seems to turn to gold?" he teased.

She shrugged her shoulders in innocence. "I guess I just have the Midas touch," she said serenely with laughter in her eyes.

"Midas touch, huh?" he said, rubbing his chin. "I'll show you a Midas touch," he said with a grin. He reached out and grabbed her arms before she could guess his intent. He was pulling her to him quickly, intent on kissing her, when her walkie-talkie went off again. He groaned as he let go of her. She chuckled softly.

"Trish, Trish, come to the guest suites stat." There was no missing the urgency in the voice that she recognized as belonging to Jeff. "Suite three, please hurry."

Trish's thoughts were racing. *Suite three. Suite three. That's the suite for Li and Kim Yee.* Fearing the worst, she ran at a breakneck pace.

David decided that she wasn't going to get away that easily this time. "I'm coming with you," he yelled as he ran to catch her.

They arrived at the guest housing out of breath. They had been on the complete opposite side of the resort when the call had come in. At some point Trish had managed to radio in that she was on her way and had replaced the walkie-talkie back on her belt. She didn't remember doing this.

Waiting for them were Babs and Frankie, whom Trish was beginning to think of as Crabs and Cranky. She was confused. *Babs and Frankie? I thought the call said it was the Yees' suite.*

Her confusion was short lived, as true to form, Crabs and Cranky were about to enlighten her.

"Director, you have *got* to do something about this!" Babs started.

"This preposterousness *cannot* continue!" complained Frankie.

"These people *must* be made to leave immediately!" they both said together. So far they had not given Trish the opportunity to say anything.

"The smell is just wretched!" whined Babs.

"And that was before this incident," Frankie added.

Finally Trish held up her hands in an effort to make them stop so she could talk. She began to tell them she would take care of it and then discovered what smell they were referring to. Trish also realized that they occupied the suite next door. She took a deep breath through her mouth and said, "Unless you can be of some help, you need to find another activity to keep you busy, something away from the guest housing or at least away from this area. *Now!*" she said with force when they did not move. The sisters hurried off.

Jeff came to the door of the suite and motioned for Trish to come in.

The smell got worse.

"Holy…" She didn't finish that statement but wouldn't have been wrong if she had. Mr. Yee had soiled himself. And by all appearances, he had been holding it in for days. Li was absolutely beside herself with humiliation that her father would do this to her. He was a grown man, after all. Trish was going to have to deal with Li's issues later. Right now she had a much bigger issue to deal with.

Michelle had also heard the emergency call on the walkie-talkie and arrived shortly after David and Trish had. Michelle was ready to help, but Trish wanted her to continue with what she was doing, to at least give the appearance to everyone else that all was normal. Trish wanted at least one of them to be visible to the general populace.

Trish did not know what to say. David had to leave the room.

Trish decided that he could help her and she could help him. She sent David to get both Dr. Mike and Nurse Katy. She told him to have them bring cleaning supplies and lots of rubber gloves.

She set about getting hot water, soap, towels, wash-cloths, and anything else she thought they would need to get the man cleaned up.

Katy and Dr. Mike arrived. The three of them cleaned Mr. Yee up, doing their best to maintain his dignity. Trish wasn't sure that he even knew what was going on. Both she and Katy had talked to him throughout the entire process, even though he never made a sound.

David was still around somewhere and made an appearance from time to time. Dr. Mike and Jeff put fresh linens on his bed. These didn't look like they had been changed either. Once they were able to reach a point where they could get the man out of his wheelchair, Trish had Jeff call one of the stable guys to take the wheelchair down to the stable to be thoroughly hosed down.

It took almost three hours, but they finally got the wheelchair, the suite, and Mr. Yee cleaned up with clean clothes put on him, fresh linens on the bed, and all of the dirty stuff placed in trash bags. Trish told Jeff to burn them all. They got Mr. Yee positioned in bed. The smell was beginning to dissipate some.

After the incident at the water park, Trish had had Dr. Mike help her do some research. He had used his connections and discovered that the old man had cancer, but they weren't sure where. Trish had Dr. Mike and Katy check Mr. Yee out completely. He was beginning to develop some bedsores, which did not help the smell any. They said they would do all they could for him, but they were not equipped for this type of wound care. Nor were they equipped to handle people in the end stages of cancer.

Sadly, Trish realized that Babs and Frankie were right. Li and Kim Yee were going to have to be made to leave the property. It was time for her to have a serious heart-to-heart with Li Yee.

After washing her hands and arms clear up to her neck at least a dozen times, Trish brought a glass of water for Li and one for herself and sat down on the sofa.

Trish was trying to figure out how to start. She was saying a silent prayer for God to give her the words.

God was watching out for her though. As she continued to sit in silence, Li began to cry. "I don't know how Father could do such a thing," she cried. "This is such a humiliation to me, to our family," she continued.

"May I call you Li?" Trish asked quietly. Li nodded her assent.

"Li, you don't really believe that your father did this intentionally, do you?" Trish asked softly. Li did not respond. "Li, your father is a very sick man. I believe that it is time for you to face the very harsh reality that your father is dying. I don't know how much longer he will be with you. I understand the hope you have that he will get better. I hope that for you too. And if that is God's will, your father will get better." There was no anger or condemnation in her voice at all, only compassion and concern.

Dr. Mike and Katy had both left after the man had been cleaned and examined. Jeff and David had both stayed in the kitchen observing, each man for his own reasons.

"Li, you cannot will your father back to health. It has to be God's design. If mere mortals had the ability to will people back to health, there would never be any illness and there would be no death.

But we just don't possess that ability. That lies wholly with God, and no one else."

She stopped for a moment to collect her thoughts. "Do you know if your father is saved? Do you know if he believes that Jesus Christ is the one true God who died on the cross so that he could have eternal life? Do you believe that, Li?" she asked quietly. "If you do believe that, then you know that when your father dies, it won't be the end, and it won't be forever. You will see him again in heaven, and he will be the father that you remember of your youth. He will be completely well with a healthy, new body, free of disease."

Li did not respond. She continued to cry softly and hold her untouched glass of water. Jeff brought over a box of Kleenex for her. She accepted them gratefully and began dabbing at her nose and eyes.

Trish was becoming discouraged at Li's lack of response. She decided she was going to have to be a little tougher on Li.

"Having him here and trying to make him participate in activities that he physically cannot do is not the solution. This is not the place for him." Still no response from Li. "We are not set up to provide that extensive of care here. He needs to be in a setting where he can be cared for by people who know how to do this, where you will have help and not have to do it all on your own. At the very least, he needs to be in a hospital. He may even need hospice care. He cannot stay here."

Li said nothing. She only cried harder.

Trish did not know if she was getting through to her or not. "Li, look at me."

When Li finally did look up at Trish, she saw only compassion in her eyes. "You have got to make arrangements for your father to be somewhere besides here. Quickly. Once you have the destination arranged, I will help you with the transportation part of it." Trish was very soft spoken, but there was no missing the authority in her voice. "Li, do you understand what you have to do?"

Li still did not say anything but nodded that she understood.

"If you need help or recommendations of any kind, please talk to me or to Dr. Mike. I'm sure he can be a very helpful resource to you."

Trish, feeling that there was nothing else to be done at the moment, left the suite. Jeff and David were right behind her. When she walked into the hallway, Michelle was just walking up again.

"You missed lunch," Michelle said, concerned. It was now after three o'clock.

Trish just looked at her. "Frankly, I'm not very hungry just now. Jeff and David also missed lunch. If they are hungry, can you work with the kitchen staff to get them something to eat?"

Michelle nodded that she would do that, though both men indicated that they were not hungry either.

Trish continued. "I'm going to my cabin to take a long, hot shower." As she walked away, she said under her breath, "I may boil my skin and stay in there for a week."

Michelle, Jeff, and David all chuckled at Trish, but Jeff and David quickly agreed that they also were going to go take showers.

Around four thirty, Trish was all bathed and wearing clean clothes and feeling much better. She had piled her hair loosely on top of her head and secured it with a single pin that resembled a chop-stick. She was considering what else to do with her hair before heading back to the dining hall to work in her office and get ready for dinner when there was a knock at her cabin door.

She opened her door to find David standing there, also in clean clothes and smelling very nice, kind of woodsy. She was surprised to see him but motioned for him to come in.

"I just wanted to tell you how impressed I was with how you handled that situation today," he said slowly as he moved to stand in front of her.

"Thank you," she said softly, lost in his eyes again. "I feel very bad for both of them. That's got to be a tough position."

He agreed by nodding but said nothing.

"Have dinner with me," he said as he reached up to wrap one of her damp ringlets around his finger.

"Well." She drew the word out slowly. "Mr. Hindley, as director of this resort, I have dinner with you every night—you and about a hundred of our closest friends," she said innocently.

"I mean just you and me, here in your cabin." He said with his finger still wrapped in her hair.

"I don't know, David." She hesitated. "I was gone all day, and I need to be visible to the guests."

"Michelle can handle it for one night. Isn't that why she is your co-director?" he asked sincerely.

He did have a point there. She was still hesitant but considering when her Nextel rang.

"Hello?"

As if on cue, Michelle said, "Hey, Trish. You know, I was thinking you've had such a nasty day. Why don't you take the rest of the evening off? I can handle things here."

"Is that right?" Trish said as she looked at David suspiciously, who only smiled innocently in return. "You're not the first person to suggest that to me today," she said.

"Good, it's all settled then. I'll see you in the morning."

Trish tried to respond. "Wait…that isn't what I said," she stuttered. But Michelle had already hung up.

Before Trish could say anything to David, who was grinning like a fool, her Nextel rang again.

"Yeah, this is Trish." She answered the phone cautiously, as if she were afraid that something might spring out of the phone.

It was Becky from the kitchen. "Michelle told us that you would be dining in your cabin tonight. We have your dinners ready. Can we deliver them to you now?"

Trish didn't miss that she had said *dinners*—plural. Curiously, she asked what they were delivering.

"For you, we have a nice steak dinner with baked potatoes, salad, and rolls, with blueberry cheesecake for dessert," Becky replied.

"You said for me. What's on the menu for everyone else?" Trish asked warily.

"Pork chops, au gratin potatoes, and angel food cake with fresh berries," Becky said cheerily.

Trish started to protest and say that she could eat what everyone else was eating, but Becky cut her off. "Tom will be there with your food in just a couple of minutes." And she hung up. Trish was left staring at her phone with her mouth hanging open.

She raised an eyebrow at David. "You turned my staff against me," she said accusingly.

"I did not turn your staff against you," he said defensively as he raised an eyebrow at her in return. "That would be hard to do anyway. They are as loyal to you as a golden retriever."

"Okay. Maybe turning them against me is too strong of a statement. But you definitely went around me to get to them."

"I just felt like you deserved to have the night off, and Michelle agreed," he said. "She helped to arrange everything."

"Everything? What everything?"

Just then, there was another knock at the door.

She opened the door to Tom, who had a cart with several platters of food. While she let Tom in, David turned on her radio and found some soft music. Tom set the food on her little table. And wonder of wonders, he also had candles. David had thought of everything.

They had a very romantic dinner. They talked more about their families. They spoke of their work. They talked of plans for the future, how they were going to see each other after the resort was closed for the summer, and what they were going to do in the meantime.

When they were getting ready to eat dessert, she asked, "How were you able to get all of this?"

"I paid one of the kitchen staff to drive to town to get it," he replied as if this were something he did every day.

"How did you know that blueberry cheesecake is my favorite?"

She had no sooner finished the sentence than she knew the answer.

"Michelle," they both said at the same time.

When they finished their meal, he took her hand and said, "Dance with me," as he led her to the little living area.

They danced in the glowing candlelight. The music was soft. He was only slightly taller than she was, and she fit against him just right. Finally, he leaned down and kissed her softly and lingeringly. And this time they were not interrupted. He tasted like cheesecake.

His deep green eyes locked on hers, Trish had been waiting for this moment. She didn't expect to feel like she did. Her knees buckled, and she felt as if she were floating. It was a good thing that David had his arms around her or she might have crumpled on the floor right there or maybe just melted into a big puddle at his feet. David didn't seem to notice that he was holding her up. Trish didn't remember ever being as happy or as content in her life as she was with this man right now.

They danced for a quite a while. And kissed often. At one point, she pulled away slightly and looked into his face. "Let's go for a swim," she said, her eyes shining with amusement.

"Okay," he said calmly. He walked over to the door, opened it up, reached out, and pulled a little sack inside.

Trish was confused. "My swim trunks," he said, smiling. Trish was still looking befuddled. "Michelle told me that there is a lake out back. She suggested that we may want to go for a swim later on," he explained.

Trish was learning that Michelle was more of a hopeless romantic than she had thought. She was also a little bit devious. Trish would have to be more cautious about what information she shared with Michelle in the future.

Trish let David go into her bedroom and change his clothes first. Then she changed into her swimsuit. She grabbed a couple of towels, and they headed out to the lake. They were the only ones out there. *Is Michelle behind that too*, she wondered.

They had been swimming and having a great time for about forty-five minutes when Jeff showed up on the banks of the lake.

He didn't see David initially.

"Trish, is that you?" he asked with concern.

"Yes, Jeff. Is there a problem?" she asked, trying not to giggle.

"No. No problem. You know, you really shouldn't be out here alone," he said with concern. "It isn't safe to swim alone."

"I'm fine, really. Thank you for your concern, Jeff. I'm not alone," she said.

About that time, David came running out of the woods and yelled, "Cannonball!" as he jumped into the lake. Trish laughed, forgetting that Jeff was even there. She turned back to David in time to see him disappear under the water. And then he was very close to her, tickling her.

They swam for a while and then went to sit on the beach and talk.

"You seem awfully young to be the director here. How did you come by this cushy job?" David asked.

"It's really a long and boring story."

"Tell me anyway. I'm interested to know." David leaned back on his elbows.

Trish looked at him for a minute to judge if he was serious or not. Deciding that he was interested, she began. "After I came to Christ, I started working at a local Christian summer camp. At first, I was just a volunteer. After I had been there for a full summer, I became a regular staff member. After I graduated from college, I became the director there. I absolutely loved it!"

She looked at him, and he nodded for her to continue. "I really loved being around the kids and getting to know them. Some campers were better than others. There was this one little girl that I just adored. In the course of the week, I learned that she and her family attended my church back home. It was really easy to keep in touch with them. When summer camp was over, I saw them quite a bit at church and still do when I can go. The little girl's mother is on the board of directors for this resort. So when they came up with this idea, the girl's mother was able to convince the others to put me in the position. I had the background and the qualifications they were looking for."

David smiled. "It may be boring to you perhaps, but it's interesting to me."

"Okay. So what about you? Here you are in the middle of this family resort by yourself. I understand that your sister was hurt, but why not cancel altogether instead of coming by yourself?"

David's smile dimmed a little but not completely. "Oh, believe me, I wanted to cancel altogether. But my parents wouldn't let me."

"And why was that?"

"My parents seem to suffer under the delusion that I work too hard and that I needed a break. You know that I work for my parents' furniture business. I have been around that store my whole life. I worked there part time doing one thing or another when I was in high school. I have been the accounts manager for seven years. In the time since I became the accounts manager, I have never taken a day off, much less a vacation. This was to be our first real vacation in more years than I can remember.

When my sister got hurt, they ganged up on me and told me that I had to take a vacation with or without them. Since they were going to make me go on vacation anyway, I decided to continue with our plans to come here. That way, I'd be fairly close to home and still taking the vacation they think I need."

"So you don't think that you needed a vacation?"

"I didn't say that. I probably did need a vacation. And I can't complain about the company." He smiled.

She smiled back. The two of them continued to sit on the beach and talk until they noticed that the lights in the staff cabins were being turned out as the staffers were going to bed.

They stood together. David said, "I'll walk you back to your cabin and gather my things."

They walked back to Trish's cabin. David collected his belongings. He kissed her lightly before going back to his own room.

Trish fell into bed that night absolutely exhausted. She fell asleep instantly. It had been a long and interesting day.

CHAPTER NINE

Trish awoke a short three hours later. She was startled awake by the sound of her walkie-talkie going crazy, her Nextel ringing off the hook, and what she thought sounded like bells going off and people screaming.

I must be having a nightmare, she thought.

She grabbed the walkie-talkie. "What is it?" she asked, trying not to sound panicked.

Someone—she didn't recognize the voice—responded, "The guest housing is on fire!" Whoever it was sounded as panicked as she felt. It was a nightmare all right, but she was fully awake.

She yanked on her standard khaki shorts, polo shirt, and shoes and sprinted out of her cabin with her hair flying unbound behind her.

Michelle was running out of her cabin too, as were the other staffers.

They all got to the guest housing about the same time. The smoke alarms were going off very loudly. They had done the job though. There were people running and screaming everywhere.

Some of the staffers went to get fire extinguishers while Trish and Michelle tried to take stock of the situation.

True there are people everywhere, but where is the fire?

Trish and Michelle could neither see nor smell smoke.

"We've got to get these people calmed down before someone gets hurt!" Trish said over the din of noise. There was no way she was going to be heard over all of the people screaming. They decided the best option was for them to start with the people closest to them and start working their way backward toward the buildings.

Trish ran to several people to her right. "Everything is all right," she said, a lot calmer than she felt. "Please don't panic. Make sure all of your group is together and go quickly without running to the open field. We will be back with you soon. Please remain calm."

She repeated this several times, as did Michelle.

After a few minutes, they were able to get the majority of the people calmed down. Hallie Atkinson was still crying, of course. Lucas and Samuel were also clinging very tightly to their parents.

The staffers had returned with the fire extinguishers and were waiting for directions. But there was still no smoke to be seen or smelled.

Trish found this very perplexing. She was also confused as to why she had not heard anything from the fire department in the nearest town. They were miles from the nearest town, but the smoke alarms were supposed to be wired to ring into the fire station. They should have at least called by now to verify the emergency.

Since they could not see or smell anything, Trish decided that they needed to split into teams and they were going to have to check each suite. She designated eight teams, one for each end of each floor of each building.

"I don't want any of you to try to be a hero. We just want to see if we can determine where the fire is and make sure everyone is out of the building. If you can see or smell smoke, get out of the area and sound the alarm on your walkie-talkie as you are leaving." She paused for a second. "You know the drill. Put the back of your hand to the door to see if it feels hot."

Michelle was to get the guest and staffing lists out of their office and make sure that everyone was accounted for. She had enlisted the help of Dr. Mike and Katy to make sure that everyone was okay, especially Mr. Yee.

Trish was on one of the search teams. She would be checking the second floor of the family housing, starting on the end closest to the dining hall.

As she went up the stairs with her team, she looked out over the people gathered in the open field; some were still crying. She noticed that in the very back of the crowd were Thing One and Thing Two. They sure looked to be having a fine old time. They could barely contain their enthusiasm. They were laughing so hard. *Why are they laughing so hard when everyone else is scared witless?*

Things began to fall into place for Trish, like fitting the last piece of a jigsaw puzzle into place.

"I think I know what the problem may be. Will you be okay without me while I go check this out?" She asked her team. They said they would be fine and they would be sure to let her know if they found anything.

Trish went back down the stairs and started across the field.

Trish was becoming angrier by the minute. By the time she reached Chris and Pat, she was in a fine mood herself. But hers wasn't so happy.

"Chris, Pat," she said. "You know, everyone seems pretty shaken up right about now. But you don't," she said very mildly. "Of course, I realize that everyone has a different way of dealing with a crisis. Perhaps yours is with levity." Her voice was not giving anything away. Too bad they didn't know her very well. They should have been able to tell by the steel gray eyes that were now looking at them that things were about to get ugly.

"You two know where the fire is?" she asked with little concern.

They both just cracked up all over again, not giving her an answer.

About that time Jeff radioed in. "Trish, we have an all clear. No smoke. No fire. All guests are out."

Michelle added to Jeff's comments, "Everyone is safe and accounted for."

Trish reached for her own unit and replied, "Michelle, have all of the guests go in the dining hall for just a few minutes, and then we'll let them go back to their suites to bed. Jeff, could you come down here with me please?"

"Sure thing, Trish. Be right there." She had them and David go in the dining hall as well, where she met up with Jeff. They were at the back of the dining hall. "Don't let them out of your site for even a nanosecond," she told Jeff.

Before she jumped up on the platform to address everyone, she checked with Michelle about injuries.

"No one was injured. They are all a little shaken, but otherwise everyone is fine," Michelle reported to her.

"Well, that's something anyway." Trish climbed on to the platform as she had done the first day and spoke to them. "May I have your attention please? Everything is under control." She scanned the faces. "There was no fire. Apparently the smoke alarms were triggered accidentally. We are not sure exactly what set the alarms off. We will have the problem looked into," she said. "We apologize for the inconvenience. We are very glad that no one was injured, and we appreciate your cooperation. You may all return to your suites at this time.

"I hope that you are able to get some rest yet tonight. We will extend the breakfast serving hours for an additional hour in the morning so that you do not have to feel rushed to get moving in the morning." She looked around the room. "Good night everyone, and again, we apologize for the inconvenience."

She started to jump down, but again David's hand was there to assist her. She barely noticed. Whereas earlier when she had been annoyed with Babs and Frankie, her eyes flashed gray, now they were a constant gray and hard as iron.

Trish spoke with a couple of other staff members on her way to the back of the dining hall. She'd had a couple of them do some checking for her.

They were able to determine exactly which alarm had been pulled: the one right in between Chris and Pat's suites. They were also able to figure out that the connection to the fire department in town had been disabled.

She told the staffers that she appreciated their help and that they had done a good job. She told them to go to bed and she would see them tomorrow.

With Michelle and David on her heels, Trish stormed back to where Chris and Pat were standing. Jeff had a hold of each one of them by the upper arm and they were squirming to get away. It looked to Trish like they had tried to leave when she told the other guests they were able to return to their suites. Jeff had not let them get very far. Jeff may have looked like he was fresh off the California coast, but he was built like a defensive lineman.

As soon as all the other guests had left the dining hall, the full extent of her fury was unleashed. "What were you thinking?" she yelled at them. They were still struggling to get away from Jeff. But he held them firm. "Do you have any idea how many people could have been hurt by this little stunt?" She didn't pause, and she didn't give them a chance to answer. "You're very lucky that nobody was seriously injured."

She paced as she yelled. With her fiery red hair long and unbound swirling behind her and her gray eyes that were hard as steel, she looked like a woman possessed.

Chris and Pat didn't even have the decency to look scared. And they certainly should have been. "Are you aware that some places prosecute for this type of juvenile behavior?" she railed.

She did stop now for just a minute to let that thought sink in. "Unfortunately, we are not set up to do that because we never thought it would be a problem."

She tried to think of what to do with them. She didn't have the staff to keep a constant surveillance on them. And she couldn't keep them in their suites. Banning them from all activities would only increase their opportunity for getting into trouble. And for the moment, at least, she didn't have a way to get them off her resort. She would have to look into that. *Until, I can find a way to get them out of here, I've got to keep them so busy that they don't have time to cause any more trouble.*

"So here is what we are going to do," she said, with some of her temper leaving her. She looked at Jeff for a second, her eyes asking him for forgiveness.

"From here on out, you will be working for Jeff. You will do whatever he tells you to do whenever he tells you to do it." She finally had their attention. They looked like they could handle anything but having to work for the large man that was currently holding them captive. "Your vacation is no longer your vacation to do with as you like. It is Jeff's and mine. You will keep staffers' hours, and you will do staffers' duties. But you will not have any of the benefits of the staffers. And you will not get paid." She was smiling now, a slightly sadistic smile. She leaned very close to their faces when she said, "And if are there any more problems, you two will be out of here so fast it will make your head spin." Both were duly frightened now. Trish wasn't sure if they were frightened of her or Jeff or both. It didn't matter as long as it worked.

She looked up at Jeff again. "They are yours to do whatever you wish with. Make them sleep wherever you want them to." She looked back at Thing One and Thing Two, then back to Jeff. "You good?" she asked.

"Yes, Trish. I'll take good care of them. Don't you worry about that none," he said with a sadistic smile of his own that made both Chris and Pat cringe.

Michelle and David had stood silent through the whole thing, but Trish knew they were both there if she needed them.

Trish sent them all to bed and went to work on the incident report and some other related paperwork in her office before finally turning in again at 4:00 a.m.

CHAPTER TEN

On Saturday, Trish was still up at six, just like normal. But she was very sluggish. She wasn't alone. Everyone seemed to be moving in slow motion today.

She rarely drank coffee or anything that contained caffeine. Today, however, she definitely needed a pick-me-up of some sort. Not big on coffee, she grabbed a Pepsi out of her refrigerator on the way to her office to get the day started.

She was thrilled to see that when she got to the dining hall, Thing One and Thing Two were busy in the kitchen making breakfast with Tom and Becky. Tom and Becky were as perky as always, but Chris and Pat seemed to be a having a little trouble functioning. She wondered where Jeff let them sleep or if he let them sleep. She was feeling better already.

Trish had found out that both Chris and Pat came from very well-to-do families somewhere in New York. Their parents didn't seem to have a lot of time for them, and as a result they were frequently in trouble. Trish wasn't sure that they had ever done any kind of real work at all. That would change if they stayed here for the rest of their vacation.

She watched them work for a few minutes and then decided that she had better get to work herself. She needed to call the members of the governing board and let them know of the incidents that had occurred last night. She didn't call them last night because it was the middle of the night. She would have to get input from them as to how they wanted her to handle things from here on out.

She also wanted to talk to them about getting some security cameras in place around the resort. They probably should have had those already, but no one had thought of it.

She closed her eyes for just a minute to prepare herself for the call. When she did, she saw green eyes staring back at her with a loving smile. She smiled reflexively in return. *I wonder if I will get to spend any time with him today.*

"Trish? Trish? Yoohoo, Trish? Are you in there?"

Trish opened her eyes to find Michelle standing in front of her, her brown eyes shining with laughter. "Did you go to sleep at your desk?" Michelle asked, smiling.

"No. I wasn't asleep. I was, however, daydreaming about a certain guest." She smiled before she continued, and Michelle was able to read volumes from that single look.

"I have to call the members of the governing board in a couple of minutes," Trish said. "Seeing David's face may be the only bright spot of my day, even if it is only in my mind."

"You know," Michelle said, "I don't think anyone would blame if you had gone to sleep. How much sleep did you get last night anyway?"

"Five hours total, maybe. That's conservative. I had a hard time turning my mind off when I went back to bed after the whole fire alarm incident." She looked over at Michelle, who was now sitting at her desk. "Why didn't we see this coming? Why don't we have security cameras in place? Why did we think that just because this is a family resort area that we wouldn't have any problems? Since we don't have anything, is it going to get worse before it gets better?"

Michelle just shrugged her shoulders and held her hands up to indicate that she really didn't have any answers either.

"How would you have handled that last night, Michelle?" Trish asked.

"I don't know. That was definitely a difficult situation to be in. I'm not sure that I would have done anything different than what you did though. I'm sure that the board will not be as hard on you as you are on yourself." When Trish looked doubtful, she said, "Don't worry about it too much, Trish. Those two are *messed up!*" clearly trying to make it Thing One and Thing Two's fault and not Trish's.

When the time came to make the call, Michelle asked, "Do you want me to stay with you or leave you alone?"

"No, you don't need to stay. I'll handle it, but thank you."

Michelle slipped out of the office and closed the door behind her as Trish dialed the number.

About half an hour later, with her call finished, Trish opened the door and found Michelle, Jeff, and David waiting for her. She emerged looking tired, her lack of sleep evident on her face. She didn't look too beat up, though, and she brightened as soon as she saw David.

"Good morning," he said as he leaned down to kiss her cheek.

"Good morning," she returned, slightly distracted by him kissing her in the dining room in front of her staff and guests.

"Well?" Michelle said, but they were all three watching her eagerly.

"They were very understanding. They didn't seem to be mad, although they did say that I have to let Chris and Pat have their freedom after dinner each night. And they have to be allowed to sleep in their suites at night. They agreed that if there are any more problems with them that I am to arrange to get them out of here as soon as possible by whatever means necessary." She paused for a moment. "And someone will be here on Monday to install security cameras in different areas of the resort.

They are also going to look into hiring security teams both to be here and to monitor the cameras."

They all continued to look at her. "Well, what are we all standing here for? I'm hungry. Let's get some breakfast," she said as she made her way to one of the tables with the other three close behind her. For the first time, the four of them ate together. They had a delightful fellowship with one another and with Jason and Megan, who were sharing their table.

CHAPTER ELEVEN

The security cameras did not get installed until Tuesday after lunch, and the security teams were not hired yet. Thing One and Thing Two had been fairly well behaved. Jeff hadn't given them much room to be otherwise. Jeff was clever enough not to keep them with him the whole the time. He moved them around and kept them separated as much as possible. While Chris was washing dishes after lunch, Pat was mucking out stalls in the stables.

Even at night there were no problems. Trish had to figure that since they had never had to do any work, they were probably exhausted by the end of the day and too tired to get into much trouble.

She and David continued to draw closer, spending nearly every evening together while leaving the daytime free for Trish to spend with the other guests.

Trish was surprised to see Li and Kim Yee at lunch on Tuesday. Though, truthfully, with everything else that had been going on, she had given them little thought. That was her mistake for not following through. She would have to pursue that.

After getting the information she needed from the men installing the security cameras, she went to talk to Dr. Mike to get some ideas about how to handle Mr. Yee, but he was with someone so she would have to check with him later. They were okay for the moment anyway. There had not been any new problems since Friday's episode.

Dinner went well. But before Trish could eat her apple pie, she was summoned to come to the laundry facility on the west end of the family building where a washer had overflowed.

She and Jeff fiddled with the thing for about forty-five minutes without success.

Trish could be considered many things. Mechanically inclined was not one of them. The best that she could do was to unplug the machine, put an out of order sign on it, and clean up the mess. She would call the repair service in the morning.

Jeff was now helping the woman who was trying to do the laundry get everything moved to one of the other facilities.

She was on her way back through the corridor between the two housing buildings when she heard a lot of commotion on the other end.

When she got to the end of the corridor, there were icicles hanging from the stairway even though it was the middle of June. What she saw in front of the gift shop made her speechless. There were Thing One and Thing Two, wearing alien heads and some kind of monkey costumes with fur and tails. But it didn't stop there. They were wearing coconut bras and grass skirts over the fur. They were both covered in frost, and there was frost and ice all over the stairs, the building, and the walkways. They had what she supposed they would call music playing and were doing some sort of techno dance.

They had clearly created a safety hazard. She was beyond angry. She was all set to round on them, but she heard something else that sounded like it needed her attention too.

She turned, looking for the source of the sound. She took a couple of steps before she ran into Babs and Frankie. They were trying to get her attention. They were yelling again.

"Director, I thought you were going to do something about them," one of them complained.

"I thought they were going to have to leave!" said the other one.

"He smells like death!" they said together.

Trish ignored them. She had heard them arguing, but she had also heard something else that she was still trying to locate, something that had her very concerned. It sounded like gasping.

She looked around. Thing One and Thing Two were still dancing. Babs and Frankie were still complaining. *Where is that noise coming from?*

Finally, she saw the source of the noise at the other end of the dining hall, near the open field. Mr. Yee was lying on the ground, his wheelchair a few feet away. And he was most definitely gasping for breath. His breathing was very noisy, and he was really struggling to breathe. She ran over to where he lay on the ground, Li standing over him crying, telling him to get up. Trish did not know why he was lying on the ground or what he had been trying to do, or rather, what Li had been trying to make him do.

Babs and Frankie had followed her and were still griping.

By now, Jeff had caught up with her, and Trish had had all that she could take.

"Jeff, turn that music off and keep an eye on those morons!" she barked. She pointed to one of the other staff members and said, "Get Dr. Mike and Katy out here *now*. And tell them to bring the oxygen." Then she rounded on Babs and Frankie. "You two, pipe down! And I don't want to hear another word from either one of you!" Her anger got the best of her. She looked around at the people who were watching everything. "Anyone else want to go a round with me tonight?" she yelled. "Bring it on!" she challenged.

Michelle, Dr. Mike, and Katy had arrived. And, of course, David wasn't very far away either. Dr. Mike began examining Mr. Yee.

"Can he be moved to somewhere more private?" Trish asked.

"Let's get him some oxygen first and then we'll see. I think his time on this planet is drawing to a close," he said sympathetically.

Great! Just great, Trisha thought. Everything was unraveling so fast. Trish had to do some quick thinking. And she made an executive decision, one that she knew she may later regret.

She let Dr. Mike and Katy tend to Mr. Yee while she grabbed her walkie-talkie. "Attention, all staff. I want every activity closed and all guests and staff members on the resort present at the east end of the guest housing units in the next five minutes for an emergency meeting. This is not optional."

The ones who were overseeing activities closed those and followed the guests back. The staff members who were not running activities were sent to knock on the doors of the guest suites and direct the guests to the meeting place.

There was still ice and frost, but it was starting to melt, creating a muddy mess.

Trish considered the events for a minute before she spoke. The guests had come to this isolated resort to get away from the pressures and busyness of everyday life, at least for a little while. Now it seemed they were trapped by the very thing they were trying to enjoy. They had come in by mass transit, and now there was no way to leave unless Trisha arranged it.

Trish stood on the ground and yelled to be heard. "We are going to make some changes. It has come to my attention that some of you are not enjoying your vacation as much as you had hoped. And frankly, I've had enough of some of the nonsense going on around here." She looked pointedly at Chris and Pat, who were not ashamed.

"Right now, I'm going to offer you the chance to leave this resort. And I don't mean temporarily. I mean your vacation is over. This is the only time this will be offered. You can decide right now to leave and be done."

She was still yelling. "Some of you will have no choice. You will be told to leave. So here's the plan. If you wish to stay, please go stand in front of the rock wall. If you wish to leave, please go to the other end of the dining hall and have a seat. Staffers, please go stand next to the field."

As people began making their way to the designated areas, she told Michelle to go speak with the people who were going to be staying. "Make sure Thing One and Thing Two are in the leaving area. And Crabs and Cranky too. I want them out of here. Make sure that everyone else understands that this is their last chance."

Michelle nodded understanding.

Trish shouldn't have worried about forcing Babs and Frankie to leave. They headed to that area on their own without prompting from anyone.

Trish walked over to where Dr. Mike and Katy were working with Mr. Yee. "Get him an ambulance ride out of my resort," she said for Dr. Mike's ears only. "Call in whatever favors you have to, but he needs to be out of here tonight. I'm not playing this game anymore." He agreed with her.

She walked over to Li and spoke with compassion. "Li, I'm sorry that I didn't see how much your denial was costing you to do what was needed for your father. It's clear to me now that you are not in the correct state of mind to make the necessary arrangements. I should not have asked you to do it. I will have Dr. Mike make those arrangements.

"Li, there will be an ambulance here to get your father shortly. Katy will stay with your father. You need to go pack your things. You *will* be ready to leave when the ambulance gets here." It was spoken softly and with compassion, but it held tremendous authority. It was not a question. It was not a statement. It was a command, and there was no ignoring that fact.

Trish was going to motion to one of the female staffers to go help Li get their things together when Jason and Megan stepped forward from their place in front of the rock wall. They told Trish that they would like to help Li gather her things. Trish started to tell them that they didn't need to do that, but she could see by the looks on their faces that they did need to do it—not for Trish or Li, but for themselves. God had compelled them to minister to this woman in her time of need. And Trisha was grateful.

Next, Trish stepped over to the area in front of the staffers. She glanced briefly at the area by the rock wall and then over to the area by the dining hall. She wasn't specifically looking for anyone. But she did notice that the Kepling sisters, the Joneses, and the Kendalls were staying, and the Atkinsons were leaving. She was more interested in the numbers. Each side appeared to be about evenly split.

She told the staffers, "Based on what I see here"—she motioned to her right and to her left—"I can let four or five of you leave if you would like to. You will be paid for the rest of this session only." She looked around. "Tom and Becky, you have to stay unless you have someone else who can take over for you."

She glanced back at Dr. Mike and Katy. "The same for you two unless one of you thinks you can do it by yourself." They looked at each other. They would both stay.

"Denise," Trish said, looking at one of the girls, "you've been pretty sick for most of this session so far. Do you want to go?"

"No," Denise said with a smile as she grabbed the hand of the male staffer standing next to her and beamed at him. "I'm not sick. I'm pregnant."

"Congratulations," Trish said, not really sure if that was a good thing or not.

She looked around at the other staffers. In the end, only three left: one girl who was terribly homesick, another young lady who had developed horrible poison ivy, and a young man who had just a couple of hours ago found out that his father had been in an accident.

Finally, Trish and Michelle walked over to address those who were going to be leaving. Trish didn't really look at the faces, her thoughts going a hundred miles an hour. Thing One and Thing Two were still wearing their monkey outfits, though they had taken off their alien heads. They were clearly not thrilled with the outcome. They should have leaned from their first encounter with Trish's steel gray eyes that it would not end well for them.

Trish addressed the group as a whole. "I don't know why each of you has made this decision and I'm sorry that you have decided to leave, whatever your reasons are. We have done everything we can to make this an enjoyable experience for you and your family."

She again had to yell to be heard over the crying of Hallie Atkinson. "I will make the phone calls and make arrangements for your departure. You will leave some time tomorrow. I will let you know the timing first thing in the morning." She paused to take a deep breath. Her throat was getting dry and irritated.

"You will receive a partial refund of your money after the inspections are completed and the fees are prorated."

She looked hard and long at Thing One and Thing Two. "You two will not be getting a refund at all. You have done nothing but cause trouble here. In fact"—she paused with a gleam in her eyes—"I have something better in mind for you. I don't want you here, not even one more night. I want you gone tonight.

"Jeff," she said, "call the sheriff. Have these two arrested for destruction of property." She smiled almost sadistically. She even handed her Nextel to Jeff to place the call.

Michelle had retrieved the clipboard with all the names of the guests and staff and handed it to Trish.

Trish was bent over the clipboard checking off the names of the people who were leaving. She had checked off Crabs and Cranky. She had marked off Li and Kim Yee and Thing One and Thing Two. She was working on the Atkinsons.

"Name?" she said without looking up.

"Hindley. David Hindley" he said sadly.

Trish's head snapped up as if she had been struck. She was once again speechless.

"I…uh…" he began.

Just then, they heard the sirens. The ambulance was coming. She passed the clipboard to one of the other staffers to finish the task as she went to speak with the ambulance personnel and Dr. Mike.

She and Dr. Mike spoke with the paramedics and gave them all of the information they had on Mr. Yee. Dr. Mike had arranged for an oncologist friend of his to be the receiving physician at the hospital, and social services had already been given a heads-up. Li was not going to be any help. Thanks to Jason and Megan, though, she did have all of their things packed.

With the exception of Chris and Pat, all of the other guests had been released to go back to their suites. There would be no activities tonight. The staff members who had chosen to leave all had their cars at the resort and had already left.

Shortly after the ambulance left, the sheriff arrived with a deputy. Trish and Jeff were on hand to speak with them about all of the stunts that Chris and Pat had pulled and to show them the latest mess.

The sheriff was a short, stocky older man with thinning hair who understood exactly the type of mischief that these two had been up to.

"Do you want them to be locked up for just the night to scare them a little and then send them home for their parents to deal with in the morning?" he asked. "Or do you want them to be arrested and fully charged?"

Trish thought for just a moment. She looked at Jeff. He was no help. He would go along with whatever Trish thought best. She hated this part of her job.

"Somehow, I get the feeling that one night in jail wouldn't change anything. Nor would the threat of being sent home to their parents. Their parents haven't done such a terrific job to this point." She looked around her at the mess. "The director and owners of this resort wish to file charges to the full extent of the law," she said decisively. "With whatever you can charge them with," she added.

Jeff nodded at her. The sheriff also agreed.

Trish wanted them out of her sight, but she also did not want to have to deal with all of their things. She spoke with the sheriff about this. It was agreed to let them each have ten minutes to gather whatever they could. The sheriff would stay with Pat, and the deputy would stay with Chris. They would not be allowed to change their clothes. After ten minutes, they would be placed in handcuffs and led off. Anything left in their suites would be for Trish to do with as she chose.

It was getting late in the evening when they finally got everything taken care of. Trish wanted to speak with David, but she still had to call the governing board. *Again.* And there was a mountain of paperwork to do, including the service order for the washing machine.

Michelle offered to help with all of the work that needed to be done. Trish refused. "Michelle, I'm the one who made these decisions. I will face the consequences. I need you to stay out of it so that we don't both fry for what I've done." She told Michelle good night.

Michelle nodded and closed the office door as she left.

When Trish finished her paperwork, she sat back in her chair, a faraway look in her eyes.

She walked up to David's suite. She was ready to knock on the door. But she realized that it was one thirty in the morning. She was sure that he was sleeping. She dropped her hand. She returned to her cabin, where she flopped on the bed and sobbed into her pillow until well after four. She finally cried herself to sleep.

CHAPTER TWELVE

Wednesday was dreary and rainy. That was fine with Trish. It fit her mood perfectly. She didn't quite manage to get up at six today. It was closer to six thirty. She was appalled when she looked in the mirror in the bathroom. Her eyes were red and swollen with big black circles under them. The bags under her eyes looked as though a family of six had decided to move in for an extended stay.

Her throat felt raw. She tried to drink some Pepsi to give her some pep and energy, but that burned her throat even more. She made some hot tea instead. That soothed her throat some. However, it did nothing for the pounding in her head. If she didn't know better, she would have thought she had been out on an all-night bender. Well, the all night part was right enough.

She went to her office to begin the process of making arrangements for those who had decided to leave. She met Michelle at the entrance to the dining hall, and they walked toward the office together.

Michelle took one look at Trish and was instantly worried. "Are you all right? If you don't mind my saying, you look awful."

"Thank you very much," Trish croaked. Even she was surprised to hear her own voice, or rather, lack thereof. She was totally hoarse.

"Shouldn't you be in bed?" Michelle asked with much concern.

"No. I have too much work to do," she whispered. "Besides, I feel fine," she lied. She honestly wasn't sure if she would ever feel fine again.

"I guess you did too much yelling last night. We need to see about getting a portable PA system of some kind so you don't have to yell to be heard as much."

Trish didn't respond immediately. Yeah, the yelling probably didn't help, but it was probably the sobbing that did the majority of the damage. "Good idea about the PA system. We'll check into it."

"What more do you have to do? And don't tell me that you don't want me involved," she whispered. Hearing Trish whisper caused Michelle to whisper too until she realized what she was doing.

"Michelle, why are you whispering?"

"Sorry. Your whispering is contagious. You hired me to assist you, and there is no way that you can do it all by yourself, especially now."

"I have to arrange the transportation to take these people out of here." She mouthed the words more than spoke them. "And then let them know the details. I also have to call a service repairman for the washer that overflowed last night."

"You do know that no one is going to be able to hear you on the phone, right?" She looked at Trish, who looked away. "I will make the arrangements and do the follow through. Don't even act like you're going to argue with me," she said emphatically. "I believe that I have the upper hand this time."

"Fine." Trisha was resigned. "I'll let you make the phone calls, but we write out the information and give it to them so there is no misunderstanding of times, places, and such. If we hurry, we can give it to them at breakfast." Trish did not want to talk to David, but she didn't want Michelle to talk to him either. *He's made his choice. And it wasn't me,* she thought sadly.

There were a total of forty-three people leaving, but four had already gone. Michelle was able to get a charter bus lined up to be on site at eleven o'clock. It would take the remaining thirty-nine guests back into town to the area where they boarded the bus in the first place. From there they were on their own.

During breakfast, Michelle got up on the platform and said, "If you are among those that have decided to leave, the bus will be here at eleven. There are fliers on the table by the door with all of the details. Please pick one up one your way out."

The bus pulled into the resort area at ten minutes until eleven. The guests were there with their bags packed. Good-byes and well wishes were said, and they were off.

After lunch, the service technician came. Trish went with him as he went to work on the washer. He found something jammed into a part of the machine that kept it from operating properly. They were able to review the tape from the security camera in the hall, just across from the entrance to the laundry facility. About twenty minutes before Trish had been summoned to the laundry area, Chris and Pat could be seen entering the area carrying an object that was found in the washing machine. They did not have any laundry, and when they left, they were not carrying anything. But they were laughing. *They set that whole thing up just to keep Jeff and me busy so that they could go through with this little stunt!* Trish couldn't believe it.

Trish called Michelle on her Nextel instead of the walkie-talkie. Trish did not want the rest of the staff to know that she couldn't talk.

"Will you stop whispering and speak up so I can hear you better?" Michelle said rather harshly without thinking.

"Michelle? Michelle?" Trish said a couple of times before Michelle finally heard her. "I'm talking as loud as I can. I lost my voice, remember?"

"Oh. Trish, I'm so sorry. I forgot for a minute."

"It's okay. I have something for you to do for me, please," Trish squeaked.

Trish had Michelle call the sheriff and add on some additional charges for Chris and Pat.

The sheriff told Michelle that he had done some checking on Chris and Pat. They had come from families where they were each an only child. However, their parents had had more money than sense and had never really spent much time with them, shuffling them from boarding school to boarding school and just generally passing them off onto whomever they could. Chris and Pat were being rebellious and attempting to get attention anywhere they could.

Trish was able to make it through the day somehow. Though, she nearly came undone when Lucas and Samuel came running up to her and hugged her legs tightly.

"What's this for?" she whispered in genuine surprise.

"You look sad," said Samuel, his dark eyes looking up at her.

"We thought it would make you feel better." Lucas smiled up at her too.

Trish was greatly moved but was able to maintain her composure. "Thank you both so much. I really did need that," she told them, willing the tears stinging her eyes not to roll down her cheeks.

Just before dinner, Michelle looked around. "Where is David? I haven't seen him around today. I would have thought that with you not being able to speak, he would be right here hovering over you making sure that you are okay."

Trish looked away for a second before she answered. "David is gone, Michelle," she said, even softer than her voice would allow. Even if she had been able to use her normal voice, Michelle would have had a hard time hearing her.

Michelle was shocked. "Why?"

Trish only shrugged and looked away. She turned away from Michelle and wiped away a tear that she couldn't stop when she thought Michelle couldn't see her.

"Are you okay? Do you want to talk about it?" she asked sincerely.

Trish again just shrugged and then indicated that she did not want to talk about it.

Michelle didn't press the situation.

Trish changed the subject. "Can you please have Jeff and a couple of other staff members meet with me after dinner? I want to start the suite inspections tonight so that the board can get started figuring out the refunds for everyone."

"Sure, I'll arrange it. Do you want me to help with the inspections?"

"No. I'll do it. You stay visible," she whispered.

After dinner, Jeff and four other staff members met with Trish in the office. She explained to them what they would be looking for. She also explained that she wanted to keep her laryngitis under wraps. She didn't want anyone thinking that she was sick and not capable of doing her job.

Trish went with two of them while Jeff headed up the other team.

Trish and her team were in Chris's room. It was a disaster. The fridge was full of junk. They had to throw everything away. The suite was going to have to be thoroughly cleaned before they could use it again. She assumed that Pat's room was the same way.

Tucked under the bed, they found a machine that they had never seen before.

"Trish, what should we do with this?" Gene asked, perplexed.

"What is it?" Trish asked just as confused.

"I have no idea. I've never seen anything like it. Could be what they used to cause all the ice and frost last night."

"Well, unless the sheriff needs it for evidence, we'll keep it. Maybe we can play around with it and see what it does. Maybe we can use it for something in the future," she whispered.

A little before ten, Jeff and his team met up with Trish and her team. "Hey, Trish, some of us have an early morning and aren't able to function on as little sleep as you do. And you sound like you should be in bed too. Okay if we call it quits tonight?" he asked.

"Which suites did you get to?" she said hoarsely before she would answer him.

After he answered, she looked over her clipboard. They only had one suite left. "Yeah, Jeff that's fine. I'll see you in the morning."

"You are not going to stay up and finish this on your own."

She raised an eyebrow at him. "Are you trying to boss me?" she croaked.

But Jeff stood his ground and held out his hand. "Come on now."

When she didn't move, he said, "Now do I need to carry you to your cabin and tuck you in, or are you going to come willingly?" There was nothing gentle about his tone. She knew that he would do exactly as he threatened.

He held out his hand again to help her as she came to her feet slowly.

"And you can't come back and finish later. It can wait until tomorrow." He led her from the area toward the staff cabins.

She wasn't sure she wanted to do the last one anyway. Maybe she would assign Michelle and some others to do it tomorrow. She just didn't know if she could handle going through David's suite.

CHAPTER THIRTEEN

When Trish had laid the inspection clipboard on her desk, Michelle saw that the only suite they had left to do was David's. Trish did not even have to ask Michelle to do it. Michelle just took care of it with Jeff's help.

The next several days and the rest of the first session were relatively trouble-free. Trish's voice had returned to normal by Friday, though she was still gravelly at times.

On Friday they learned that Mr. Yee had passed on just the day before. *Thank you, Father God, that we got him out of here in time!* Trish thought to herself.

The majority of those who had remained were largely those people who had flown under Trish's radar during the first half.

And without problems around every corner, Trish found that she actually had more time to spend with the guests and engage in the activities. Several of the guests thanked her and let her know how much they enjoyed the resort and the opportunity that it provided.

That was good. It helped for Trish to stay busy. It gave her mind less time to wander to other areas. It tended to wander of its own will sometimes anyway. She spent a lot of time with Lucas and Samuel and the Kepling sisters.

Sometimes her Nextel would ring. The caller ID showed that it was David's number. She would not answer it. When she would go back to her cabin at night, she would see that she had some missed calls on her personal cell phone. They were from David too. She did not call him back.

After the end of the first session, the remaining suites were inspected and things were being readied for the next group.

Of the three staff members who had left with the other guests during the first session, only one would not be returning, the young lady who was so homesick. The young man's father was home from the hospital and recovering nicely. He encouraged his son to return to work. The other young lady was feeling much better after having been put on some steroids for the poison ivy. She returned to work with additional medication in tow in case she got it again.

The staff had four days off to do whatever they wanted. They could go into town or play at the resort or whatever.

During one such day off, all of the staff had decided to go in to town for the day. They were going to go eat and then go to a movie.

Trish had decided not to go with them. Both Michelle and Jeff had volunteered to stay with her, but she wouldn't hear of it.

"No. No, you guys go and have a great time."

Trish was surprised to hear a car pull into the parking lot not long after they left. She was beginning to question the wisdom of staying there alone. *I haven't seen the security guards lately. How far away are they?* she wondered.

She walked around the corner of the dining hall cautiously, not really sure what she was expecting to find.

A huge smile spread across her face. She was delighted to see an attractive, older version of Michelle step out of the car.

"Nan, what a great surprise!" she exclaimed as she ran to greet Michelle's mother, Nancy. "You look great as always. But Michelle isn't here though."

"I know, dear. She called and told me that they were all going into town. And that you were staying back by yourself." She hugged Trish tightly to her for a moment and then held her at arm's length to look at her face. "I came to see you."

Trish nodded slowly. Her eyes were full of sadness. She recovered quickly. "Well, come in, come in. Can I get you something to drink?"

Michelle's family had sort of adopted Trish. Nancy had become the mother that Trish never had. Their bond was special even though they were not related by blood. But Trish had never felt comfortable calling her Mom. And Nancy thought that "Nancy" was too formal for their relationship. So they had settled on Nan. No one called her that except Trish, not even Nan's husband, Jerry.

When Nan felt that the time had come, she suggested that Trish show her around the resort area. "How about we go for a walk?" she asked patiently.

They walked in comfortable silence for a few minutes with Trish pointing out various parts of the resort occasionally.

Nan deliberately slowed their pace as she asked, "So how are you? You look pale and tired. How much weight have you lost?"

Trish didn't answer right away and looked off into the distance. She shrugged her shoulders to indicate that she didn't know how much weight she had lost. Her cheeks were flushed and her eyes were sad. The bags under them had become a permanent fixture. When she spoke, her voice broke. "It's so hard. I had never felt the way he made me feel before in my life." She looked down at the ground as she said softly, "And I've never felt like this before either."

Nan put her hand on Trish's arm. "Michelle told me that you wouldn't talk to her about it. I knew that your hurt must be really deep for you to not even talk to Michelle." They came to a bench and Nan motioned for Trish to sit. "Will you tell me?"

Trish sat and almost immediately started sobbing with her face in her hands. "Oh, Nan, what is wrong with me? Why does everyone leave me? What is God punishing me for?"

Nan put her arms around Trish and drew her close. She let Trish sob for several minutes, handing her Kleenexes that she had put in her pocket.

It wasn't so much that Trish couldn't talk to Michelle. It was more that Trish didn't feel free enough to show her vulnerability to anyone with her staff so close by. She was supposed to be the one in charge. And she couldn't be in charge in her current state.

Nan just stroked her hair and held her while she cried. "You go ahead and cry. It's okay, honey."

"I don't understand, Nan. Why am I so unworthy to be loved by anyone?" Trish continued to sob.

"You're not unworthy, sweetheart," she murmured. "Jerry and I love you as much as we love our own kids. Michelle loves you. And you know that all of her brothers adore you," she said.

"You're just saying that," Trish cried. "If that's the case, why does everyone leave me? I shouldn't have been surprised that David left me. Nobody ever stays in my life once they get to know me. I'm as worthless as my mother said I was."

"You know that God loves you above all others. He will never leave you or forsake you. That's His promise to you." She tried to look in Trish's face. "Trish, look at me."

Trish raised her head slowly, her eyes red and swollen.

"Did you hear what I said? God will never leave you. Never. He doesn't say the road will be easy. But regardless of how hard it gets, He will always be right there with you."

"Then where is He now?" Trish asked sincerely.

"You know as well as I do that just because we can't see Him doesn't mean that he isn't here and working in your life. He is hurting because you are hurting."

Nan looked into Trish's eyes to make sure that she was getting through to her. "Your mother should never have said that to you. Not just because it was mean, but because it was wrong. She was wrong. You are not worthless. You are many things, but worthless is not one of them." She looked at Trish again. "You are a beautiful, smart, funny, and successful woman. I've never met anyone with more determination than you have. For your mother to have said those things, clearly she did not know her daughter. Any man will be lucky to have you. You have such a big heart, and your capacity to love despite your childhood is astounding."

Trish's sobs were quieting now. But she had the hiccups. "Then why—*hic*—did David—*hic*—leave me too?"

"I can't answer that. The only people who know the answer to that are David and God." She held Trish's hands now. "Have you talked to him?" she asked.

Trish shook her head. "He's tried to call a few times. But when I see his number, I ignore it. He hasn't called recently."

Nan looked sympathetic. "I know how badly you must be hurting, but I don't think it's wise to assume that he left because of you. Since you have not spoken to him, you have no idea what may be going on his life. It could be that he is just as miserable right now as you are."

Nan continued, "I'm sure that God has someone special in mind for you, someone who will appreciate the very special woman that you are. It could be that that person is still David. It may be someone else altogether. Either way, no matter what you do or don't do, God can still carry out His plans for your life. But you have to let Him have the reins."

Trish nodded. She was feeling better. Having Nan here was a huge balm to her heart. Even though Trish had cried the very first night when she had found out that David was leaving, she had not talked to anyone about it. All her thoughts of being worthless just continued to fester in her mind until she believed every word that her mother had said. She knew now that that was Satan wreaking his own brand of havoc on her heart. She had needed to hear the godly words that Nan had spoken to her. She thanked God for Nan. She also thanked God for Michelle, who had had the wisdom to call her mother when all else had failed.

CHAPTER FOURTEEN

The second session of the summer went much smoother. Everything was pretty routine, and Trish didn't have nearly as many problems to deal with.

They had gotten a portable PA system. That made making all of the announcements easier. Trish didn't have to yell to be heard.

The security teams and cameras were up and running like they were supposed to be. This also took a lot of the stress off of Trish. She didn't have to be the policeman in addition to being the director. But there hadn't been any problems this go-around anyway.

And last she had heard Chris and Pat were still in jail. The governing board and owners had agreed wholeheartedly with her decision to press charges.

Some of them even came out to the resort the next day to check all the damage that had been done. They had no intention of letting Chris and Pat off the hook for this.

The guests as a whole were a lot friendlier to be around than the guests during the first session had been. That did not make her miss David any less though. He did not try to call her anymore. She was, however, getting through it one day at a time, trusting that God had a different plan in mind for her. Her color was improving, but she had yet to regain her weight. Her appetite still was not normal for her. She looked sickly.

Trish's biggest challenge this session was how to deal with one family in particular who had a daughter who was physically challenged and confined to a wheelchair, Missy. She was fourteen. She had been born with a birth defect that left her legs fairly useless, but the rest of her was fine. Missy had it in her mind that she had to be able to try to do everything. Her mind was sharp as a tack, but her body was not capable.

The differences between Missy and Mr. Yee were immense. For starters, Missy was able to talk and carry on a conversation. She was so animated and full of life, whereas Mr. Yee was never even conscious. Missy had an all-terrain power wheelchair. It could also be switched to manual mode if need be. Missy went everywhere in her wheelchair. She was able to maneuver her wheelchair on the trails and everywhere else.

Trish tried for several days to protect her. She didn't want to see Missy get hurt. Missy was really a delightful girl, and the rest of the family was very nice also. After a few days of Trish trying to tell Missy's family that she couldn't do something only to be proved wrong, Trish gave up trying to restrict Missy's activities. Missy's family clearly knew what she was capable of far better than Trish did.

It didn't take long for Trish to get to the point where she was looking forward to seeing what Missy could do every day.

Missy was afraid of nothing. She even convinced Trish to race her up the rock wall. Trish agreed, thinking this girl wasn't even going to be able to get off the ground. She should have known better.

Trish decided that she would take it easy on this girl so that her feelings would not get hurt. Trish seriously underestimated Missy's upper body strength. The first time up, Trish was left in the dust while Missy flew up the wall. The second time up, Trish held nothing back. She gave it her all. Missy still beat her, but not by as big of a margin.

Now Trish knew how David had felt when she beat him at everything. *David? Where had that thought come from?* She tried to push it out of her mind.

As the summer continued, Trish received an invitation to Jason and Megan's wedding to be held in September.

She got several letters from Annie and Bridgett Kepling. Bridgett had really come out of her shell in the time she spent at the resort and from all reports was continuing to do so. Annie was thrilled.

Finally, in August, the second session and the summer came to an end, just in time for school to start. The guests had gone. The staff would be leaving soon—some going back to college, others going to different jobs.

Trish and Michelle would be staying on with the company to prepare for future sessions.

One day, after all of the guests had gone, Trish and Michelle were tying up loose ends before they moved back to their office in the city. Trish had been out at the main activities venue checking on some things.

She returned to the office and immediately saw Michelle. "Michelle, I think we only—"

Michelle was not alone in the office.

"David." Her heart tripped, and her breath caught in her throat.

She turned to leave the office, but before she could, Michelle jumped up and ran to the door. "I'll just be going now." She left quickly and closed the door behind her.

Trish tensed and tried to pace away from David, but the office was just too small and there was no room.

"Trish, I would really like to talk to you."

"I don't have anything to say."

"Maybe you don't, but I do."

She kept her back to him.

"Are you always this stubborn?" he asked softly, but there was no heat in it.

She didn't answer.

"Okay. Fine. Look I handled my leaving very badly. I'm sorry."

She continued to keep her back to him, but her stance had relaxed some.

"I am crazy about you. My life hasn't been the same since that very first day that I arrived at the resort and saw you with your red hair. You are an amazing woman, and you fascinate me to no end."

Trish blushed to the roots of her hair. She whirled to face him now, restless and agitated. "Then why? Why? Why did you leave me that way?"

David took a deep breath. "I hadn't planned to. I really hadn't. I was in the space over by the rock wall, planning to stay. And as I watched you with Li and Kim Yee, I realized that I missed my family terribly. And I also realized that life is so, so short. I was just overwhelmed with the need to see my family and tell them that I love them. And before I knew it, I was in the area over by the dining hall preparing to leave that beautiful resort and the beautiful woman that I had come to care so very much about."

He placed his hand on her cheek. "Won't you give me a second chance?"

She closed her eyes and breathed in the scent of him. "I was hurt. I was very hurt. I guess that I wasn't very fair to you either though. After I found out that you were leaving, I went out of my way to avoid you. I didn't want to talk to you."

She looked up for just a second before she continued. "I've never felt the way I do when I'm with you. But every person that I have ever cared about has walked out on me and never looked back. I figured that you were just another one of those. And I didn't want to give you the chance to talk to me, to tell me what I already knew, that there is something horribly wrong with me that makes it so that nobody can love me."

"Is that really what you think?" he said gently as took her hands.

"It was. I do understand why you left. I should have given you the chance to tell me. I'm sorry." She looked at him with tears in her eyes.

He kissed her lightly. "If you give me the chance, I promise I won't be one of those people who walks out on you."

In September, Trish and Michelle met with the governing board to discuss changes, what worked, what didn't. The first session taught them all a lot. Missy taught them a lot too. And after the way things had gone during the first session, Trish was very grateful that they had even decided to keep her, much less ask for her input into how to make things better.

They decided that they were no longer going to offer six-week-long sessions. They were going to have ten-day sessions. Apparently, it was the consensus that six weeks was not only too long to spend trapped with your family, it was too long to spend trapped with someone else's. And ten days seemed to be the magic number.

"So what do we do with the staff in the meantime?" Michelle had asked.

They talked about it for a while, and finally it was decided that the staff would have two days off in between each session to keep them from getting too restless.

But Michelle wasn't done yet.

"I'm sorry for being so bold," she started apologetically, "and I know that Trish would never complain. That's not her nature."

Trish was glaring at Michelle now, having no idea where Michelle was headed.

"I'm not sure if you are aware of this, but the events of this past summer were very hard on Trish—physically, mentally, emotionally. There were some days that I was extremely worried for her well-being."

By now, Trish was positively red with embarrassment. She continued to glare at Michelle, all the while wishing that the earth would just open up and swallow her whole.

One of the board members looked at Trish with great concern. "Oh. We didn't realize. Are you sick? Are you not up to continuing?"

"I'm fine," she said through gritted teeth, burning holes into Michelle with her eyes.

Michelle at least had the decency to be embarrassed. "That didn't come out at all the way that I meant for it to. Trish is perfectly capable of handling the job," she added quickly.

She looked flustered for a minute. "What I meant was that Trish feels that everything is her responsibility. Sometimes she tries to take on more than she can handle, and she doesn't ask for help. Every time there was a problem, she would spend hours trying to handle it herself. There were frequently times when she would stay up until three or four o'clock in the morning taking care of things and then be back at it at six. She truly was on the job twenty-four-seven all summer long."

"Is this accurate?" one of the other members asked.

Trish slowly nodded her head and looked down at the table.

"Not to mention the months of time she put in before we opened. And she hasn't stopped yet. What I am trying to say," Michelle continued, "is that when you put that kind of time and commitment into something, when you put that much of yourself into it, it wears on you."

The members looked at each other and nodded in agreement. "So what are you proposing, Michelle?" they asked.

"I think she should be made to take a break, like halfway into the summer. You know, like a week's vacation away from everybody else's vacation?" she said timidly. "I can handle things long enough for her to be gone for a week. And there are other staff members there who could help me out so she that she could take some time off."

"Trish, we are glad that you enjoy your job and are doing your best. We have been very pleased with how you have handled things so far," the first board member said, looking at Trish with something close to pride. "But we did not realize that you were putting so much of yourself into this. Michelle is right. It isn't healthy for you to do so. It isn't healthy for anyone. Everyone needs time away from their job sometimes. They need to be able spend time with their families and to pursue other activities."

The board was all staring at her now with concern. Michelle was looking very pleased with herself. And Trish couldn't find anything to say.

"You will take a vacation during the summer, and Michelle will be in charge while you're gone." The board member looked at Michelle now as he spoke. "If she does not leave voluntarily, please call me and I will personally come and get her and remove her from the resort. Trish, will you cooperate with us on this?"

"It doesn't seem that I have much of a choice," she said resignedly. "But if I have to take a vacation, Michelle does too."

It was Michelle's turn to look embarrassed.

"Michelle?" the woman said.

"That sounds fair enough," she said.

They discussed some other things, and Trish was relatively quiet.

"If we are not going to have the six weeks' sessions, is there something else that we can do with the grounds when they are not being used during the rest of the year?" Trish had eventually asked, finding her voice again.

This opened up the discussion in a whole new avenue. The board members had not given this much thought until just then.

They tossed ideas around about this too. They felt that it would be a good idea to open the resort for fall break, winter break, and spring break. And they were going to offer up the resort to churches and youth groups for retreats and activities. But the activities would not be so elaborate.

Someone had figured out how to work the machine that was taken from Chris's room. It was indeed the device used to create all of the frost and ice on their last night. They planned to use it to make an ice skating rink.

There were two changes that would affect every guest over the age of eighteen. Every adult would have to have a full criminal background check and authorization from a physician that they were healthy enough to participate in all activities. The governing board had already put these into the agenda before their meeting with Trish and Michelle. But Trish was extremely relieved by this. Hopefully, they wouldn't have any more problems like what they experienced during the first session.

And thanks to Missy, they were going to bring in consultants to make the place more handicap and wheelchair accessible. They were even going to try to have a special session set aside just for those people who were physically challenged and their families.

The meeting finally concluded, and Michelle and Trish drove back to their office in silence.

Michelle was the first one to speak. "You know that I only said what I said because I love you and I am concerned for you, right?"

"Yeah, I know, but I was still embarrassed," Trish replied.

"Trish, you are my best friend. I don't want anything to happen to you. And there are others who think that you work too hard. You *do* work too hard. That's not a surprise to you, right?"

"Me? I work too hard?" Trish tried hard not to smile and to look shocked. She didn't quite pull it off.

CHAPTER FIFTEEN

It was the middle of October. Trish was finally on her way home from work. It seemed that everything that could go wrong today had. Trish had meeting after meeting to attend, and everyone was long-winded today.

Trish had met with the consultants at the resort to discuss the changes that needed to be made to make the place more wheelchair accessible. The meeting had lasted way longer than Trish had anticipated.

On top of that, Michelle had called her earlier in the day and told her that the latest physical forms were ready for Trish to inspect and hopefully give her approval on. So she still had to stop by there to talk to the forms people.

She finally arrived home a little after six thirty. She was well and truly beat. She had been too busy to eat something. She was hoping that she had something in the freezer or cabinet that she could heat up.

She unlocked and walked partially in her front door. She noticed immediately that something was not right, but she could not put her finger on it. Someone was or had been in her house. She didn't go any further than the foyer. Trish stood with her hand on the doorknob, the door not completely shut so that she could run out again if she needed to. She got out her cell phone and prepared to dial 911.

She called out. "Michelle?" No answer. "If there is someone here, you should know that I have a gun, and I'm not afraid to use it." *Really? Didn't they say that in all of the movies?* Actually, she did have a gun. Unfortunately, if there was someone in the house, he would probably shoot her with it, as it was in her nightstand drawer. "I'm calling the police now," she yelled.

David walked slowly out of her kitchen with his hands up.

The two had been dating for two months. Since that day in August when he had apologized to her, he was really trying to prove to her that he was not going to walk away from her. They frequently would meet for lunch somewhere or have dinner after work. He was always surprising her with little things, trinkets or flowers or just a quick text message to let her know that he was thinking about her. And with each little surprise, Trish felt herself falling more in love with him.

And with all of those surprises, she really shouldn't have been so surprised to find him coming out of her kitchen.

Her heart was already beating frantically from the adrenaline at the thought that someone was in her house. Seeing David did nothing to calm her racing heart. She slowly lowered her cell phone and closed the front door.

"David? You scared me to death. What are you ... I mean, how did you get ..." She had become incapable of speech again and was looking back and forth between him and her front door. She was sure that it was locked just now when she came in.

He was standing in front of her wearing a long-sleeved denim shirt over a plain white t-shirt and blue jeans. And a devilish smile on his face. Good night, he was handsome! David reached into his pocket and pulled out a key that he let dangle from his right hand.

Trish knew in an instant that Michelle had been involved. She was the only other person who had a key to her house. Come to think of it, Michelle had scheduled her entire day. *Just how involved was Michelle?*

Trish recovered quickly. Relieved that it was David and not someone meaning to harm her, she started toward him.

She stopped when he motioned to someone else.

A woman stepped from the kitchen around the corner closest to Trish.

Trish was a little startled. "Who are you?" she asked hesitantly.

"I am Claudia. And for now, I am your personal assistant."

Trish raised an eyebrow at David, who continued to smile like the cat that ate the canary.

Claudia continued. "Miss, if you will please come with me. Your bath is waiting."

"My bath?" Trish looked at David again and then followed Claudia into her own room where there were candles lit everywhere. In the bathroom, Trish's garden tub was filled with hot, soapy water loaded to the brim with bubbles. Claudia began to help Trish undress. Trish felt uneasy about that. "I can undress myself."

"As you wish," Claudia said. "Take as long as you like. I will be here when you finish to help you do your hair and dress."

Trish was thinking she was in a time warp or something. *A maid to help me dress and undress and do my hair?* Trish sank into the hot water with bubbles up to her chin and felt the tensions of the day start to float away. She didn't know what David was up to, but she couldn't have argued with him if she wanted to.

She didn't remember the last time that she had indulged in a luxurious bubble bath. She lingered in the tub for over half an hour. When she was finally ready to step out of the tub, Claudia was there as promised.

Claudia wrapped a huge, thick, warm towel around Trish as she stepped out. Trish had never seen that towel before. She started to push Claudia away until she felt the warmth of the towel. She looked at Claudia with confusion on her face.

"It just came out of the dryer," Claudia said, as if she could read Trish's mind.

Trish dried herself, and then Claudia led her into the bedroom where there was a little black dress lying on the bed with a pair of matching shoes on the floor. *Where had those come from?* They weren't there when she entered the bedroom with Claudia the first time. And they certainly were not hers. But as she put them on, it was as if they had been made just for her. They fit perfectly.

Claudia did her hair. It was a simple upsweep. She basically piled it loosely on top of Trish's head with loose tendrils hanging down. It was secured with a single pin.

"What am I getting so dressed up for?" Trisha asked.

"Why, dinner, of course," Claudia answered easily with a smile.

When Trish was dressed, Claudia led her back out to the living room.

Trish was again surprised by what she saw there.

There were more candles. The dining room table had been moved into the living room and sat in front of the fireplace, which had a nice fire roaring within it. The table had been covered with a beautiful white, lace tablecloth and was set with fine china. Trish didn't think that she owned any of this stuff either. There were more candles on the table. There was soft music playing.

David was standing in front of the fireplace, his back to her.

He turned and she saw that he had changed clothes too. He was now wearing a tuxedo complete with a bowtie. His green eyes were sparkling. If Trish thought he were handsome earlier, her heart was nearly tripping over itself at the sight of him now.

He stepped up to her and took her hands in one of his. "You are so beautiful," he said as he wrapped a fiery tendril around his finger.

He motioned for her to sit down. He pulled her chair out for her and then helped her scoot it in.

"What is this all about?" Trish asked him.

"You have been so busy the last couple weeks that I've hardly seen you."

"Oh, David I'm so sorry. We're trying to get things ready for fall break."

"I know. I know. You don't have to apologize. I wanted to see you and do something special for you. I'm sure that you didn't eat anything."

She looked faintly embarrassed as she looked down at the table.

"I enjoy pampering you."

He nodded to someone, and a man brought out a bottle of wine.

Trish was growing more and more confused. *Who is this man, and where did the wine come from? This is my house, isn't it?*

"You pamper me more than I deserve" she told him.

"Oh, I don't think so." He kissed her hand.

He stood up and went over to her and pulled her up from her chair. He took her face in his hands and kissed her gently. "I adore you."

She nodded and turned her face into his hand and kissed it. "Well, thanks for that."

They sat back down, and David motioned to the kitchen. Claudia and the man who had brought out the wine earlier now brought out their dinner, all her favorites: steak, baked potatoes, salad, rolls, and blueberry cheesecake for dessert.

They enjoyed their dinner while talking comfortably. After dessert, he again stood and held out his hand and said, "Dance with me."

They danced closely, absorbed in the nearness of each other. While they were dancing, Michelle, who had been directing the activity from the kitchen, Claudia, and the man who had brought out the wine slipped quietly out the door, unnoticed.

After several minutes of dancing, he kissed her again.

"My parents would like for you to come with me to their house for Thanksgiving," he told her.

She looked shocked. "Thanksgiving with your parents?" Her voice went up an octave. "But that's still a month away."

"Relax. It'll be fine. My mother likes to plan ahead. They really want to meet the woman who has me so distracted so much of the time."

"Am I supposed to take something?" she asked.

"My mother said that was up to you. She doesn't want you to feel pressured."

"I'll think about it," she said.

"Don't worry about it. Anything that you make would be great."

"You're just saying that hoping I'll cook for you again."

He grinned hugely. "You caught me. I love it when you cook for me."

They continued to dance for a while longer, and then, as she was hoping that this night would go on forever, he took her hand and led her to the front door of the house.

"It's been a long day for both of us." He lifted her hand to his lips and kissed it gently. "So I think it would be best if I go home now." He kissed her again gently.

He walked out the door and she watched him leave. When she could not see him anymore, she closed and locked the door. But she did not move. She leaned against the door and sighed deeply.

CHAPTER SIXTEEN

Trish slept later on Saturday morning than she usually did.

Trish couldn't wait to talk to Michelle and tell her everything that had happened, though she suspected that Michelle may already know a great deal of it since she had arranged all of Trish's schedule the day before and had let David into her house.

She was still in bed, thinking that she would have to call Michelle, when the phone rang.

"Hello," she answered sleepily.

"Hey, girlfriend," Michelle responded. "I just wanted to tell you not to touch the kitchen—"

"The kitchen?" Trish cut her off. "What's wrong with my kitchen?" Trish asked confused.

"Don't worry about it. I'll be over later to clean it up for you."

"What are you talking about?" Trish asked. But before Michelle could respond, Trish figured it out.

"You were here last night?"

"Yes. I was kind of directing things so that David didn't have to worry about it. I stayed in the kitchen out of the way."

"I didn't even see you," Trish said.

"That was the idea," Michelle replied sarcastically. "Like you would even notice me with the handsome Mr. Hindley in front of you anyway.

"How long were you here and what did you hear?" Trish asked curiously.

"I left when you started dancing, and I heard absolutely nothing. I kept my fingers in my ears the whole time," Michelle said.

"Sure you did. Hey, listen, I'll clean the kitchen myself. Do you have lunch plans?"

"No. Not really. Mom said something about a movie later, but we haven't carved that into stone. You want to get together?"

"Could you meet me for lunch at that little café near the office, say twelve thirty? I would really like to talk to you."

"Okay. Do I get hint about what's up?" Michelle asked a little concerned.

"No. You will just have to wait until lunch." And with that she hung up, leaving Michelle looking at the phone for answers that weren't going to come.

They met at the little café next to their office at twelve thirty.

Trish was the first one there. She sat at a booth and looked over the menu while she waited for Michelle to arrive. She wasn't really looking at the menu. She was too nervous. She didn't need to look at the menu anyway. She and Michelle came here for lunch all the time. She knew that menu like she knew the back of her hand.

Michelle came in and sat down. "So what happened last night after I left?" she asked curiously.

Trish looked away and took a drink of her water. But before she could say anything, the waitress came up to take their order.

"I'll have the turkey club with a bowl of potato soup," Trish said as she handed the menu back.

"Can I get a Caesar salad and a glass of tea, please?" Michelle said.

The minute the waitress walked away, Michelle looked at Trish expectantly. "So?" she prompted.

"David's parents want me to come for Thanksgiving."

"You sound surprised. So are you going to go?"

"I am surprised, and I don't think that I have a choice," Trish said.

"Why? Surely, you knew that eventually they were going to want to meet you. And you always have a choice. You know that you could always come to our house again."

"Yeah, but…" Trish looked out the window for a minute. "It still blows my mind that David is interested in me. Now his parents want to meet me too? I guess I did know that this would happen eventually, but I didn't expect eventually to be so soon."

Michelle just laughed. "They are going to love you, just like my parents do. And besides, David will be there too. He isn't just going to throw you to the wolves."

They both looked up as the waitress delivered their food.

"So, if I don't come to your house, will you and your parents just be totally crushed?"

"My dad will be terribly disappointed. He is still waiting for you to realize that you are madly in love with one of my brothers," Michelle said.

"Am I? Which one?"

"I don't think he much cares. Any of them."

"Is that because he wants me in the family or he would like to get one of your brothers out of the house?"

Michelle laughed. "Both, I think."

"I don't know what to tell him about that. But unless I'm wrong, he might be losing one of his kids to marriage soon anyway." She looked pointedly at Michelle. "So how is Jeff these days?"

Michelle's face brightened immediately. "He's fine."

"You're beaming," Trish teased. "And you talk about me. You've got it just as bad as I do."

"You're right. I do."

"So what are you guys doing for Thanksgiving?"

"Jeff is coming to our house. But he has already met my family so it isn't as big of a deal."

"He's met your brothers and he still wants to come back? Hold onto him with both hands."

Michelle laughed again. "That's my plan."

The two continued to talk and eat until Michelle got a text message from her mom.

"Hey, Mom wants me to go shopping with her and maybe see a movie. Want to come?"

"Sure. I'll come." Trish signaled to the waitress that they were ready for their check, and the women left the café.

CHAPTER SEVENTEEN

David picked Trish up at eleven o'clock on Thanksgiving Day. She was a bundle of nerves.

"Do I look okay?" She fussed with her sweater.

"You look just fine. Now will you quit worrying?" He leaned over and kissed her lightly. "Are you ready?"

"Yeah, I think so. I just need to grab the sweet potato casserole and the banana bread."

He followed her in to the kitchen where they picked up the food items. He helped her carry the food out and got her settled into his car.

"I don't know if that food is going to make it to my parents' house. That bread smells wonderful."

"Thanks. I just took it out of the oven about an hour ago."

They arrived at the Hindleys' home just a few minutes later. It was a large, brown two-story house with beautiful landscaping and a large yard. Trish could easily picture little kids running around, playing in the yard.

They walked into the house, and Trish was enveloped by the heavenly smells coming from the kitchen.

The whole family was there to greet them as they walked in.

"Trish, this is my dad, Steve, and my mom, Pam. Mom, Dad this is Trisha Sterling."

Trish was all set to shake their hands and found herself in a warm hug with each of them. "It's a pleasure to meet both of you. You can call me Trish."

As soon as Trish was released from her hug with David's father, she felt someone trying to help her out of her coat. She turned to see a younger David standing there. "You must be Todd. I've heard a lot about you." He also hugged her as soon as she was out of her coat.

And last was Chelsea. She was short and had the build of a gymnast. Her shoulder-length hair was the color of rich honey, but she had the same vivid green eyes that David and Todd both had.

"Come in. Come in," said Mrs. Hindley. "There isn't any reason to stand in the foyer and talk when we've got this big house. Please make yourself at home."

Trish followed David into the living room, where the tail end of the Macy's Thanksgiving Day parade was playing on the television. Trish looked around the room. It was well decorated in warm and inviting colors.

"Mrs. Hindley, your house is just lovely. I love how you have decorated it."

"Thank you, Trish. Please call me Pam."

"Trish, we are so glad to finally get the opportunity to meet you. David talks about you quite a bit," Mr. Hindley said.

Trish blushed. "Don't believe anything he says, Mr. Hindley. Unless it's all good and then you can believe all of it."

"Steve," he said. "We're not big on formalities around here. We want you to feel welcome and comfortable in our home."

Todd jumped in. "David said that you beat him at nearly everything when he was at the resort. I want to hear all about it."

David groaned. "I knew I shouldn't have told you that."

"Did you really beat him on the shooting range?" Chelsea was suspicious. "David has always been such a good shot."

"Chelsea, who are you kidding?" Todd asked. "David can't hit the broad side of a barn."

David chucked a throw pillow at his brother, who dodged it easily.

Trish answered each of their questions. She didn't feel at all like she was being interrogated. The conversation was easy and comfortable.

As it came closer to time to eat, when Pam got up to go to the kitchen, everyone else followed, including Steve, David, and Todd. Trish watched as the family moved together like it had been orchestrated that way. Chelsea got the serving platter out while David took the rolls and the sweet potato casserole out of the oven. Steve began carving the turkey while Pam mashed the potatoes. Todd set the table. They all worked together to set out the remainder of the food.

Todd said grace, and they enjoyed a wonderful meal.

Trish couldn't believe how accepting his family was of her. They, too, took her in and loved her as one of their own, especially David's sister. Chelsea loved having another female around. Trish was quite enamored with her too. She had the best time with them. They were so fun and loving. They really made her feel like family, just like Michelle's family had.

After dinner, when all of the dishes had been cleared away, the four kids went out to the yard and played football. It was David and Chelsea against Todd and Trish. At one point Trish got the ball. She was trying to dance around David when Todd saved her. He didn't just block for her; he tossed her over his shoulder and ran with her toward goal.

"You wouldn't dare tackle me while I have your girlfriend," he yelled to David over his shoulder.

Trish was laughing the whole time. She never let go of the ball, and she and Todd scored the winning touchdown.

Later, they played board games with the football games on in the background.

"Trish, are you coming back at Christmas?" Chelsea asked.

"Do you want me to come back at Christmas?"

Steve answered. "We would love for you to come back at Christmas. You are always welcome here."

"We would like for you to come on Christmas Eve and stay with us for the night so that you are here on Christmas morning. We have an extra bedroom." Pam said.

"I appreciate the offer, really, but I wouldn't want to impose. I don't live that far from here. I can come over on Christmas morning if that's what would you like."

"David's apartment isn't far from here either, but he will be staying with us on Christmas Eve," Chelsea said.

Todd spoke up. "It's not imposing if we invite you."

Trish could not argue with that. Plans were made for Trish to come on Christmas Eve.

"Speaking of Christmas," Steve said. He handed Trish a simple silver ornament and a package of permanent markers.

Trish held the ornament and looked at it, the markers, and the man with confusion.

"We have a tradition in our family," Steve said.

Pam continued. "Instead of buying fancy ornaments for our Christmas tree, we like to have our friends and family decorate our tree for us."

"The important people in our lives are given an ornament with a package of permanent markers," Todd said.

"You can decorate the ornament any way you wish, with whatever you want. The only rules are that you have to put the year and either your name or initials on the ornament somewhere so that we know who the ornament came from," Chelsea told her.

"You want me to decorate an ornament for your Christmas tree?" Trish looked around at all of the faces that were watching her.

"We not only want you to decorate an ornament for our tree, we want you to be the first one this year." This came from David as he put his arm around her and smiled down at her.

It was all Trish could do not to cry. She felt so special.

CHAPTER EIGHTEEN

On the morning of Christmas Eve, David again picked Trish up. She was not nervous this time. She had been over to David's parents' house for dinner several times since Thanksgiving. She still did not understand why they wanted her to come so early though. She knew they wanted her to go to the candlelight service at church with them. But beyond that, she was clueless.

They arrived around noon, and Pam had a small lunch on the table for them.

Trish noticed that the oven was on.

"Isn't it a little late for a cookie exchange?"

Everyone laughed. "We aren't having a cookie exchange," Chelsea told her. "But we are making cookies."

"Since David was a small boy, we have always made chocolate chip cookies on Christmas Eve as a family. We used to make them for Santa, but now it's a tradition," Pam explained.

"That's part of why we wanted you here so early, so you could be part of some of our family traditions," Todd told her.

"What are some of these traditions?" She was a little leery.

Everyone started talking at once. Trish laughed at how excited they all were.

"Well, we'll go to church at six for the candlelight service. And we'll go out for dinner afterward," Steve said.

"Dad, don't forget the presents," Chelsea added. "Before we go to church, David, Todd, and I, and you of course, will open one gift from one of the others."

"You open your gifts on Christmas Eve?" Trish asked.

"No. No. Not all of them. We only open one," Todd said. "I might choose to open the one from David or Chelsea or you. The rest wait until tomorrow."

"After dinner, we will come home and make a big bowl of popcorn and watch *The Christmas Story*," Steve said.

"*The Christmas Story?* Is that a movie about the nativity?" Trish asked.

"Have you never seen *The Christmas Story?*" Todd could not believe it.

"No. I don't think I have. I don't watch a lot of TV, and family traditions were not something my family did."

"It's all right, dear." Pam said. She drew Trish to her side. "We'll make up for lost time."

"So what is this movie about if it's not about Jesus's birth?"

"It's about—" Chelsea started.

"I don't think we should tell her." Todd cut her off. "You, Ms. Sterling, will just have to wait and see."

He had a smirk on his face that Trish didn't quite trust. But he was absolutely adorable. She could see why he always had girls around him. His smile was brilliant, and he was very much a rogue.

They had a great time making cookies. Pam had to tell Todd and David repeatedly to stay out of the cookie dough. Trish laughed. The boys ended up with flour all over the place. But they cleaned it up with just one look from their mother.

The kids opened their gifts. Chelsea got a pink sweater from Trish. Todd got a new wallet from

David. David got a steering wheel cover for his car from Chelsea. And Trish got a small bottle of perfume from Todd.

Trish really enjoyed the church service. And they had a nice dinner afterward. Trish snuggled on the couch against David during the movie. She loved the movie and laughed at David and Chelsea as they threw popcorn at each other.

She was further surprised when she got ready to go to bed and both Steve and Pam stood and gave her a hug before she went upstairs. They told her to sleep well. She didn't remember anyone ever having done that for her before. They also told her that she absolutely could not go downstairs before seven in the morning. She found this statement very confusing but agreed that she would not.

Trish went to bed that night tired and excited. She usually went to Michelle's family's house on Christmas Day. She had never experienced Christmas Eve like this before.

Trish awoke on Christmas morning feeling disoriented. It took her a few minutes to remember where she was. She heard what sounded like giggling and people talking very excitedly. She looked at the clock. It was 6:57. There was a soft knocking on the door.

"Trish," someone whispered. "Trish, are you up yet?"

She rubbed her eyes. "Ummm. Yeah. Give me just a minute." She looked for her robe. She tied the belt as she opened the door. There in front of her with huge smiles on their faces stood Chelsea, Todd, and David.

"What are you doing?" she asked.

"It's almost seven. It's almost time to go downstairs," Chelsea informed her.

"Time to go downstairs?"

"Yes. We can go down at seven." Todd told her.

She thought they might be kidding her, but she couldn't be sure.

David didn't say anything. He just stood there watching her with a smile on his face.

She wasn't entirely sure she understood. Before she could ask another question, Chelsea grabbed one hand and David grabbed the other. They half dragged her to the stairs with Todd following in their wake. They were not kidding her. They really were as excited as kids for Christmas morning.

When they reached the living room, Trish was amazed by what she saw. It looked like the gifts from the night before had multiplied overnight. She even had a stocking hung up with her name on it. She hadn't noticed that the night before. After the way the other three had acted upstairs and dragging her down the stairs, she almost expected them to just dig into the gifts and to see paper flying everywhere. She was starting to feel a little that way herself.

She was shocked when, instead, they turned back toward the kitchen. The four of them immediately set about brewing coffee and making a big breakfast. Trish was having the time of her life.

Steve and Pam came down stairs at eight. Breakfast had just been put in the oven. They took turns opening their gifts, the smell of eggs, Danishes and coffee wafting through the house.

Trish could not believe how many gifts there were for her. She got some very nice things, including some leather gloves and some things to decorate her house with. David got her a pretty bracelet that had gems the color of her eyes in it. She got David a new iPod.

The kids had timed things perfectly. The timer on breakfast sounded just as they were throwing away the last piece of trash.

Throughout the day, people came and went with a constancy that Trish found alarming. There were cousins, aunts, uncles, grandparents, friends, and neighbors. But they were always greeted warmly with hugs and, "You're just in time." Trish wasn't quite sure what they were in time for, but everyone was "just in time."

Trish understood that David was a special man and that he came from a special family. The Hindleys had a knack for making everyone they came into contact with feel welcome. They loved everyone. They shared their blessings generously, and they never forgot what Christmas was really about.

She thanked God for bringing this man and his family into her life.

EPILOGUE

Not long after the first of the year, Trish and David had gone out for dinner after work. During their dinner, David asked her, "What would you say if I were to ask you to marry me?"

"I would say...put your money where your mouth is."

They both laughed as they had had this conversation several times. He would ask the question during conversation, but there was no follow-through.

They finished their dinner and walked out to the car. It was terribly cold, and they were waiting for the car to warm up before they left the parking lot.

David said again, "What would you say if I were to ask you to marry me?"

She was trying to think of an answer that she hadn't given him before when she noticed that he was reaching into his pocket.

Before she could respond, he spoke. "Trisha Sterling, will you marry me?" He presented her with a simply elegant ring that was just her style.

Her hands flew to her mouth. She started crying and somehow managed to squeak out, "Yes. Yes."

Trish and David were married in early May. The ceremony was held at the For the Love of Family resort in the open field just outside of the hiking trails.

The landscaper had spelled "good luck" with red and white impatiens.

All of the staff from the resort was there. Denise was there with her new baby that everyone cooed over.

Even some of her previous guests were there. Annie and Bridgett were there, and so were Missy and her family. The Joneses had been invited as well but were unable to attend because Daphne had found out that she was pregnant again, and the pregnancy was not going well.

All of David's family was there—aunts, uncles, cousins. David's brother was his best man.

Michelle was Trish's only attendant. Michelle was wearing a pink strapless sundress with a white bolero. She was positively radiant, sporting a shiny new engagement ring of her own. Jeff was all smiles too.

The setting in which Trish and David were married was beautiful, but not nearly as beautiful as the bride was.

If Michelle was radiant, Trish was stunning. Trish wore a white strapless sundress with a little pink bolero. Her hair was done in David's favorite style, the sun shining off of it giving it a golden hue. She carried a bouquet of miniature pink roses sprinkled with baby's breath.

Michelle's father, Jerry, gave her away. And even he couldn't keep the tears from his eyes as he answered the minister that he and Nancy gladly gave this woman to this man.

The ceremony itself was simple, the way they both wanted it. Trish and David wrote their own

vows. Nearly every one in attendance was crying happy tears by the time it was all over, as they promised to love, honor, and cherish each other all the days of their lives.

But this was just the beginning. David was taking her to Italy for their honeymoon for two weeks. She was due back at the For the Love of Family resort at the end of May.

Trish was happier than she had ever been in her life. She knew that no matter how bad things got this summer, she wouldn't be alone. She would have David to lean on for support.

And from here on out, it really would be for the love of family because for the first time in her life, God had given her a family to love.